The Miracle of Alvito

To Dora + Frank —

Very Warm Regards —
(+ Happy Anniversary Again)

Dave Branden
3 Sept 2008
Los Altos

The Miracle of Alvito

And Other Stories

David H. Brandin

Author, *The Horns of Moses, A Novel*
Co-author, *The Technology War*

This is a work of fiction. Names, characters, places and incidents either are the product of the author's imagination or are used fictitiously, and any resemblance to any actual persons, living or dead, events, or locales is entirely coincidental.

Publisher Information

Copyright © 2008 David H. Brandin
Los Altos, CA 94022-2121
author@thehornsofmoses.com
http://thehornsofmoses.com

This book was printed in the United States of America.

To order additional copies of this book, contact:
Xlibris Corporation
1-888-795-4274
www.Xlibris.com
Orders@Xlibris.com
46315

Contents

For Ellen

"[N]ot even a Swallow could fly over Rome"
—Italian Fascist Grand Council, 1943

" . . . [A] woman is only a woman,
but a good cigar is a smoke"
—Rudyard Kipling, *The Betrothed, ca.* 1885

"God is an Integer"
—The Pythagoreans

Acknowledgements

Illegals © *2008 Cigar Magazine,* Reproduced by Permission, First Published as *Illegals: A Chapter in the Life of a Trafficked Cubano Family, Cigar Magazine,* Fall, 2008

Cesspool Charlie, co-authored with Reuben Greenspan (1904-1988)

Four Stars © *2007-2008* David H. Brandin, Modified and Reproduced by Permission of Author, First Published as a scene in *The Horns of Moses,* iUniverse, Lincoln, 2007

Information about Bull Sharks in *TIGER!* Drawn From *Wikipedia: http://en.wikipedia.org/wiki/Bull_shark*

Baggage cites *The Sirens of Titan*, Vonnegut, K., Delacorte Press, 1981

Foreword

After retiring from a career in computer science, I began writing fiction in September of 2006 and completed the last story in this collection in April, 2008. Along the way, I published a novel, *The Horns of Moses* and began development of two new books, *The Earthquake Prophet* and *Symbolic*. Both future books are non-fiction.

This collection, written over an eighteen month period, includes historical fiction, science fiction, fantasy, and even some truth masquerading as fiction. It's an eclectic collection; there are no underlying themes or philosophical messages embedded in the stories. However, all the pieces have an unusual twist—an unexpected ending. Some of them spoof the modern world, a few contain political satire, and some examine information technology conundrums. Each deserves a few words.

The Miracle *of Alvito*, for which this collection is named, is a World War II story that is based, to some extent, on an actual event in the town of Alvito, Italy during the bloody battle for Cassino. It's a love story as well as a tale about war. The underlying basis of the story is true, and as a result of events in the war, the town changed the historical name of a church to The Church of the Miracle.

Illegals is a fantasy story about trade in illegals. It is the first story I ever sold and it was first published in the Fall, 2008 issue of *Cigar Magazine.* Some liberties are taken with the law.

Baggage, a science fiction story, considers what happens when airlines misplace people, instead of baggage. It was inspired by Kurt Vonnegut's *The Sirens of Titan.*

A Sure Thing considers the question: What is gambling? Is it gambling when the results are predetermined? When there is no risk? Can there be machines that are more or less logically equivalent to slot machines, which do not constitute gaming devices? Under such conditions legal chaos might ensue.

Coolidge Said, is based upon a saying attributed to Calvin Coolidge. The story examines the problem of erasing data stored on computers and in networks. It is fiction but the underlying technological issues are real.

The Piano Police is fiction. A small boy is terrorized by his piano teacher for not counting the notes—a story that will be familiar to any music student. The story was inspired by Stephen King's *The Library Police.*

Gravity, perhaps my shortest and favorite story, is science fiction. An inventor, based on a not-so-implausible assumption about Einsteinian physics, develops a gravity pump. The consequences are rather unpredictable.

Four Stars is political fiction in which the director of a military agency encounters an aggressive legislator. Political satire, it is not difficult to imagine such events today. The story was drawn from a scene in *The Horns of Moses*.

Tiger! is a scuba diving story based upon true events in Fiji; a partially fictionalized story about a Shark Feed that went astray.

Big Numbers Are LARGER Than Small Numbers considers the question of what transpires when complex numerical concepts serve as the focus of a criminal trial. This story is, perhaps, the most complex technical tale in the collection. Still, it is a good introduction to irrational numbers and other concepts of number theory—a good algebra background would help. It's fiction, of course, but the mathematics is correct.

Data is a fictionalized account of a real courtroom hearing in which a county tax assessor attempts to tax the data base of a company. A pompous computer scientist examines the difference between computer programs (which tell computers what to do) and data (which the programs work on). Sometimes, the reader will discover, there is considerable ambiguity between the two.

That Room will be appreciated by fledgling writers. Semi-true, it describes the experience of a writer, as he "pitches" his concept for a new book to a publisher and agent at a writers' conference.

Top Secret examines the problems facing a person with troubling family history issues when he applies for a Department of Defense top secret clearance. In the interest of full disclosure, polygraph examinations are normally reserved for higher level clearances but incorporated into the story.

Ben and Greta is a love story. Originally written as a scene for *The Horns of Moses*, the vignette was removed to reduce the number of characters in the novel.

The Greatest Roman—Ever asks: What If Cicero, the greatest orator in Rome were really an idiot? Based on actual events in Rome during the political maneuvering before the second Roman civil war, this historical fiction story examines the perspective of the major contenders such as Caesar, Mark Anthony, and Octavius (Augustus).

Day of Infamy is a spoof about the origins of a war. The reader will discover that Japan and America have fought more than one war.

Cesspool Charley was originally written by my uncle, Reuben Greenspan (1904-1988), when he lived in Death Valley. I revised, completed, and edited the story. It considers what happens when a dynamite expert is hired by the man who stole his woman. I included it in this collection because it met my standard for an unusual twist at the end.

The Test is fiction, based on identity theft. In this case, a man steals his own identity which surely is the easiest identity to steal. The thief, an arrogant and angry man, has some interesting adventures.

Writing short stories is fun. One takes a real life experience (usually their own), rumor, innuendo, mixes in some fiction, and caps it off with an unexpected ending. But I had help. Sylvia Halloran and her students in a Creative Writing class in Los Altos, California offered invaluable feedback about these stories; Martha Alderson, author of *Blockbuster Plots*, beat discipline into me; and Lou Fried, my friend and author of *Other Countries/ Other Worlds* inspired me. Bob Martini, whose family comes from Alvito, provided considerable background on the town of Alvito. And my wife, Ellen, suffered all the indignities of a writer's wife—endless proof readings.

Good reading!

David H. Brandin
Northern California
2008

The *Miracle* of Alvito

June 2, 1944

It rained that day—the day of the funeral—hard! Angels may weep but this was a downpour. The Italians called it a *diluvio*. Water pooled in the church graveyard and streamed into Piazza Marconi. Yet the entire population of Alvito had turned out to honor the dead man. The people listened reverently to the young priest as he delivered a eulogy. They watched as the gravediggers pounded down the dirt on the grave, and the priest's sister laid a funeral bouquet. They watched as the rain ravaged the flowers and turned clumps of dirt into red mud. They watched as the dead man's friend and the German prisoner stood at the grave and saluted. The townspeople were wet, hungry, sick, and worn out from war, but they stayed as the deluge continued. They'd witnessed a *Miracle* and they prayed for the dead man's salvation.

May 8, 1944

1:30 PM

Surrounded by ridges and large mountains to the east, Alvito was a small town of the Valle di Comino on the edge of the National Park of Abruzzo. With roots to the Roman Empire and Dictator Sulla, the town had been established circa AD 1000. It was one hundred miles southeast of Rome in the province of Frosinone—fifteen miles north of Cassino, the closest large city. The population was small, more typical of Italian mountain villages. Its name could be traced to the Latin *Olivetum*.

The battle for Cassino was underway. After Mussolini had been sacked the Italian government fled south. The Germans had occupied northern Italy and the Americans and British had landed forces on both sides of the southern Italian Peninsula. Field Marshall Kesselring had deployed *XIV Panzer Korps* to stop the allies at Cassino. German troops had also occupied Alvito, astride a secondary, but strategic, crossroads in their supply route.

Father Eugenio Martini, twenty-six, was the town priest. He was a small man five feet six inches tall, with a ruddy complexion and an intense personality. He'd recently taken over church duties when Father Antonio D'Auria passed away. He'd taken it upon himself to protect Alvito from the occupiers. Although some townsfolk thought it was collaboration to do so, he'd cultivated his relationship with the German garrison commander, *Herr Oberst* Hermann Küchler. The priest was surprised he actually liked Küchler, a thirty-five year old Bavarian. Perhaps, he thought, it was due to the *Oberst's* education in philosophy. Küchler was a cultured and refined man who seemed to hold the Nazis in contempt, although he rarely said anything explicit. The two men were on a first name basis when others were not within hearing distance.

Sitting in the sunlight with his new friend, Father Martini told himself that collaboration wasn't bad if it saved lives, and besides, the Pope was a master at getting along with the Nazis. And Pope Pius XII's real name was Eugenio Pacelli; another Eugenio, so how bad could it be? Martini's older brother, Roberto, thirty-six, who owned *La Farmacia*, had urged him to cooperate with the Germans, "We must save the town." His younger sister, Isabella, sixteen, had been critical and vitriolic, "How can you talk to these monsters?" She was a hot-headed Italian beauty and he'd hoped she wouldn't cause trouble. Their father Antonio, the old mayor had equivocated, worried about how the partisans might react.

Martini was having lunch with Küchler in the Piazza Marconi when one of Küchler's men, *Korporal* Wandt, rushed onto the piazza and turned the hand-cranked siren on Küchler's command vehicle, parked nearby.

"Here they come again," said Küchler. "Perhaps it's us this time."

"*Herr Oberst*, they're bombing because your forces are here. You're an educated man; you've studied Kant and Schiller; why can't you just put up a white flag?"

"Are you mad, Father? General von Senger would shoot us all, and, if he missed, my knowledge of the philosophers wouldn't protect us from the *Führer's* wrath. The *Gustaf* Line protects the *Adolph Hitler* Line to the west. If it fell, can you imagine the storm that Berlin would unleash? The allies would take Rome. Surrender is out of the question."

"*Herr Oberst*, you know the war is lost. The Americans have landed at Anzio; the British have taken Ortona. They'll cross the mountains soon. Your cause is hopeless."

"Of course, Father. It's been futile since those fools in Berlin decided to invade Russia. But I'm not a suicidal man, we're talking about survival. We have to bear up and, please, try to keep your people and the partisans calm; I'm doing my best to avoid reprisals, but if the battle heats up in Cassino we may get visits from the SS."

"We need to think of something. If the bombs come any closer the town will be destroyed."

"I'm surprised we haven't been hit already. Headquarters tells me the entire province of Frosinone is being bombed."

"I'll pray tonight to San Valerio, our patron saint, for both of us."

"If I recall, Father, San Valerio was a Roman soldier."

"He was canonized for making people feel worthy and healthy. He represented the good that soldiers bring, instead of the evil of war. His bones were transferred to Alvito from Rome in 1656 to protect the people from plague. We hope they will protect us from the bombs."

"That would be nice Father," said Küchler, "but for the moment we'd best go to the shelters. It would be wonderful if your God would end this crazy war—but don't tell anyone I said that."

Both men headed for the shelters and the bombs narrowly missed Alvito, falling south toward the bridge over the River Mollo. Father Martini wondered what the real target was; every day the bombs marched closer to Alvito. Perhaps, he thought, the bridge was the target today. The Mollo was a tributary of the Melfa, which flowed into the Liri River. The Liri River Valley dominated the northern approaches to Cassino and could serve as an invasion route for allied forces. Martini knew that Küchler had long feared the Allies would eventually attack the bridge. Küchler had set up his anti-aircraft guns on its approaches. Father Martini hoped the problem wasn't complicated by partisans—or the SS, he thought, pray those barbarians never arrive.

May 9, 1944

3:30 AM

A U.S. Army Air Corp C46 transport, on a northern heading and painted black for night runs, flew over the Liri River. Large peaks loomed in the east. The countryside was jagged with small mountains and ridges that separated tiny valleys. At three thousand feet, the wind shredded the cloud cover, and the light from a full moon glinted off the surface of countless lakes, rivers and streams. The transport's door was open and the jumpmaster had turned on a red lamp, which indicated the aircraft would be over a drop zone in one minute. Standing near the door were Captain Carl Rugby and a squad of four U.S. Army rangers. Rugby, twenty-six, was a short, wiry man who'd been raised in a rough neighborhood in Philadelphia. He'd studied cartography at the University of Pennsylvania. The slipstream whipped past his face.

"Okay," yelled Rugby, "Jameson with the BAR goes first, then Allen with the explosives, then Weiss with the radio, then you, Michalak, with the spare radio; then me with the extra weapons. Clear?"

"Bullshit, Captain. I hate explosives—*beep*—and I especially hate jumping," shouted PFC Allen, with a nervous shudder. Allen had seen a lot of combat and he'd developed a nervous twitch that manifested itself with an accompanying beep, which sounded like a loud hiccup.

"Yes, Private," said Rugby. "Thanks for volunteering. Any other comments? Don't whisper!"

"Yes sir, Captain," said twenty-two year old Staff Sergeant Ray Michalak. "Thank God I'm not jumping with the explosives. I got to carry a radio." Michalak was tall, with a dark complexion and wavy brown hair.

"Screw you, Ray!" shouted Allen, which earned him a smile from Michalak.

"Quiet down, Allen," commanded Rugby. "Pay attention; we need the explosives. Jameson, you keep that Browning Auto ready to cover the drop zone. And you're right, Michalak; if we can't blow the bridge on the Mollo, we need the radios to send traffic reports. You and Weiss better not mess up! Now get ready!"

The jumpmaster triggered the green lamp and Jameson, Allen, and Weiss jumped in sequence. Michalak was almost out the door when a twin-engine Messerschmitt 110 *Zerstörer* interceptor, one of the few serviceable German night fighters in the theater, came directly out of the moon. Armed with two twenty mm cannon and four 7.92 mm machine guns, it pounced on the C46. Twenty mm cannon shells struck the rear of the cabin. The shells left gaping holes in the fuselage and just missed the two rangers and the jumpmaster. One shell damaged the rudder. The Messerschmitt pilot knew that *Luftwaffe* combat doctrine dictated that he finish off the transport, but the three parachutists were too tempting. The *Zerstorer* came about to attack them with its machine guns. Exploiting the opportunity, the C46 pilot pulled the yoke back, threw the throttles forward, struggled to control his yaw, and raced for safety in the clouds above. Just before the transport entered cloud cover, Rugby and Michalak saw their men get raked by machine gun fire and the demolitions exploded in a burst of flames.

"Tough luck, Captain," yelled the jumpmaster. "We're miles north of the drop zone and you've lost half your squad. We can't outwait that fighter. With this damage we got to get home. Do you still want to jump?"

"We go, now!"

Michalak jumped, followed by the captain.

As he drifted down, Rugby watched Michalak below him and thought back to the meeting that had cost him three men. It had been the previous week, in Naples, with a Fifth Army G2 major.

"Captain," the major had said, "Fifth Army has a tough one for you. We want you and your rangers to blow the River Mollo Bridge south of Alvito, and then report on German reinforcements in the Liri River Valley."

"If I read the map correctly, that's a secondary supply route to Cassino."

"Correct, We're routinely bombing the main road south from Rome, Highway 7—the old Appian Way—and Highway 6, the alternate route, is unusable—it's been flooded by German engineers to protect the northwest approaches to Cassino. But the Germans are occupying Monte Cassino, the high ground, at the old Benedictine abbey—it's the anchor of their *Gustaf* defense line. We need to take that mountain. Get the bridge and we damn near close their supply routes."

"It looks like the mountain dominates all the valleys north including the Liri. I thought we'd bombed the abbey to rubble."

"We did and we're getting a lot of flak in the press for that. The damn thing was built in the Sixth Century. But the Fourth Indian Division requested the bombing after taking heavy casualties. They thought German artillery spotters were up there. No one knew for sure but German paratroops occupied the place after the bombing, in any case."

"But I'd heard that Kesselring ordered the site to remain unoccupied and that he'd informed the Allies."

"That's right. General Clark wasn't convinced the abbey was occupied. He demanded a direct order to authorize the bombing from the theater commander; British General Alexander—and he received it."

"So the Abbey was destroyed and the Germans ended up on the high ground anyway?"

The G2 major shook his head in disgust and pointed back at the map. "The place is criss-crossed with rivers and streams and, with the spring rains, it should really mess up German reinforcements to Cassino. I can't say when, but there's going to be another major assault."

"How many assaults will that make, Major?"

"Four."

"Jesus," Rugby had said. "What are the casualties?"

"Intel figures the Krauts have suffered fifteen thousand. We've taken over forty thousand. That includes us, the Indians, Brits, and others."

"Hopefully we won't add to the total." Rugby paused, eyeing the major who seemed to be too casual about such horrendous casualties. When he saw nothing in the major's eyes, he added, "Okay, understood. I've got good men. We'll do our best. The *Gustav* Line and Cassino are the keys to Rome, and maybe Italy."

"Yeah. Still, Kesselring has another set of fortifications about twenty miles west of your drop zone, called the *Adolph Hitler* Line. But you're right, Cassino is all about Rome. Happy hunting and good luck."

In the moonlight, Rugby and Michalak were still about thirty feet in the air when a strong gust of wind snarled Michalak in his parachute shrouds. His chute collapsed and he struck the ground hard, with an ankle at an awkward angle. Rugby was right behind him on the ground.

A crest of hills lay between the American soldiers and the River Mollo. They could see the ruins of an old castle which cast long shadows in their direction. There was a road on their right that worked its way east, toward San Mario del Campo and the Appennino Mountains. The area seemed deserted.

"Shit, Captain," said Michalak who clutched his ankle in pain. "Those guys were my buddies."

"Yeah, I know." Rugby grieved over his losses. Allen was a smartass, but he knew his demolitions. Jameson was a rock, and Weiss was a musician with Morse code; they were all damn good men. Three more dead, he fumed, for that G2 major. The good news, if there was any, was that Michalak could tap a key too.

He shook his head clear and looked at the distant ruins. It was the *Castello* just north of Alvito. He remembered it from his briefing. It had been constructed at the end of the Eleventh Century and rebuilt after a major earthquake in 1349. The Borgias had lived there. It was pretty far away and he figured he'd look around the town for a closer hideout.

Turning to Michalak he said, "I'm going to miss all of them. But now we got to think about us. I guess we can forget about the bridge. What about your ankle? Is it broken?"

"It sure feels broke but at least it ain't bleeding. I might be able to hobble if we splint it. It hurts like a bitch, though. What're we gonna do?"

"I don't know. We got to get under cover before daylight. Maybe the *Castello,* if we can get you there. But that'll take a lot of time. That German pilot is going to report a drop was underway."

"If you help me crawl into the bush, I'll report in while you come up with some ideas."

The captain dragged Michalak into a thick clump of bushes, stashed the extra weapons, and helped him set up the radio. "Use the battery and remember—no more than one minute on the air."

Michalak nodded. "It really hurts, Captain. Can I have some morphine?"

"I've only got two ampoules of morphine in my kit. Do you want one now?"

"Tell you what, Cap. Give me one of the shots and I'll inject it after I transmit; it could knock me out for some time."

"Okay." Rugby applied a sloppy splint to the sergeant's ankle with a stick and some parachute shrouds and buried the rest of the parachutes.

"Thanks, Captain. How about getting me a beer while you're out there?"

"Listen up, Ray! One minute. We don't need them triangulating us with direction finding equipment. I'll check out the road. If we can find a place to hole up, we'll see what we can do about the ankle. Weiss had the first aid kit and we're going to run out of morphine."

"Okay." Michalak paused and tried to get comfortable as the captain checked his weapon.

"Hey, Captain, you speak the local lingo?"

"No, but I speak some German. My grandparents were immigrants from Germany and I'm pretty good."

"Shit, we sure don't want you speaking German to anyone."

"Let Fifth Army know what happened."

Ninety minutes later, as dawn broke, Rugby returned. He shook Michalak awake. "The whole town is occupied by the Germans. We better spend the day in the bushes. Did you make contact?"

"I reported our casualties and that the best we can do is monitor traffic if the Krauts don't get us. But the battery crapped out at the end. We'll need to use the crank."

"Okay. It was sooner or later. Relax now. We'll figure out something later. I can give you another shot in the afternoon.

The men spent the next twelve hours hiding in the dense underbrush and watching an occasional German patrol drive by.

May 9, 1944

6:00 PM

Isabella Martini had placed a quarter wheel of cheese, a few bottles of the regional wines, and a small assortment of meats in the church cart. It was a cool evening and she'd thrown a shawl over her shoulders. She and her brother, Father Martini, were late for their weekly supply trip to the Franciscan *Convento di San Nicola,* located on the road toward San Mario del Campo.

They were hitching the church's horse to a cart when *Herr Oberst* Küchler appeared.

"Eugenio, you're a little late to be visiting the *Convento*, aren't you?"

"I had to give the Sacrament to old Baglio, the butcher. He's quite ill. His son was adamant that I come this evening."

"Father, if I were a believer I would insist upon you for my last rites."

"One would think a Bavarian would be a religious man. Would you like to come with us tonight? You can drive. I believe," he smiled with mischief in his eyes, "our horse speaks German."

Küchler laughed and looked at Isabella, whose nostrils flared. She had made it clear to the whole town what she thought of the Germans. They were all the same, barbarians—even this one, who was educated in philosophy. She knew Küchler was appraising her and she didn't want to give him any encouragement. She flashed her eyes at her brother and looked away.

"No, Eugenio," said Küchler, with a disappointed look. "Go with your God and please don't get in trouble. You're the only person I can talk to south of the Alps. *Schöne Reise*, Isabella."

"*Arrivederla*," said the priest.

Isabella nodded and said nothing.

Twenty minutes later, on Via Colle Civita, Isabella and Father Martini were startled by a soldier who barred their way, rifle in hand. His face was blackened and he wore an American flag patch on his shoulder.

"*Chi è?*" asked the priest. "*Che vuole?*"

"Excuse me, Father," said the soldier. "Do you speak English? I'm sorry to interrupt your journey but there's a war on, you know."

"You're American? What do you want?" Martini spoke in lilted English.

"Captain Carl Rugby, U.S. Army Rangers. I need some help. I have an injured man with me and he's in pain."

"Are the Americans here? I thought they were fighting south of Cassino."

"They still are, Father."

"Captain, do you know that the Germans are everywhere around here? When will the rest of your forces get here?"

"I've seen the German patrols. I don't know when we'll be relieved, but I urgently need to move my man and find a place to get under cover before dawn. Can you help?"

"Of course. But I need to deliver these supplies to the *Convento*—"

"I'll stay," volunteered Isabella, in English. "My name is Isabella. Perhaps I can help." She smiled at the American captain.

Father Martini said, "She's my sister, Captain. I will hold you responsible for her care. When I return, it will be after dark and we'll hide you and your man in the church cellar."

"Thanks, Father. I guess I can trust you to return, seeing as how you're leaving Isabella behind."

As Father Martini drove off, Rugby escorted Isabella off the road. They found Michalak pale, feverish, and semi-conscious.

"He looks like he's in shock," said Isabella. "We need to keep him warm and elevate his legs—even the one with the splint." She took off her shawl and draped it over the sergeant.

Some moments later Michalak opened his eyes. He looked at Isabella and saw a beautiful young woman with large hazel eyes, long black hair, and a willowy figure. He blinked several time.

"Captain, I asked for a beer and you brought me an angel!"

Isabella smiled and began to flush.

"Take it easy, Sergeant," said Rugby.

"Now, Sergeant, please," said Isabella as she examined his ankle. "You have a broken ankle. We will need to re-splint it later and that will be very *doloroso*, er . . . painful. I recommend you rest now."

"Are you a nurse? What's your name?"

"I've had some training at the *Convento*. That is where I learned my English too." She was unsure whether she should give her name to the handsome soldier.

"Her name is Isabella," said Rugby. "His name is Ray, Isabella."

Michalak settled back; his head cradled in Isabella's lap and smiled up at her. Her heart skipped a beat and her flush deepened; she wondered if it were apparent that she was flustered.

As they waited for Father Martini to return, Isabella thought of her brother, the priest. This was the first time she'd been proud of him since the Germans had arrived. He'd have to deceive them now; she wondered how he would deal with that.

May 9, 1944

10:30 PM

Under cover of darkness, Rugby and Michalak were spirited into the basement of the church, *La Parrocchiale di San Simeone*. It had been built in 1700 to house the patron saint San Valerio's bones. Rugby thought it was an impressive baroque structure and the priest told him the ceiling was gold trimmed.

As they carried in the sergeant, Rugby asked the priest why the Nazis hadn't looted the ceiling.

"Captain, for the last three years Italy was an ally of Germany. Fortunately, the local German commander is a civilized man. I hope he doesn't learn we're hiding you here. He would have to do something about that."

"Look, Father," said Rugby, "we'll need to use a radio from time to time. I hope they leave us alone, too."

"I will pray for that," said Isabella. They laid the sergeant on a long table in the cellar and she began to reset the splint on his ankle. He was in serious pain but didn't utter a sound. Rugby could tell from Michalak's silence that Isabella had captured the sergeant's heart. She seemed unsettled and the captain sensed an attraction for Michalak; he hoped it wouldn't be a problem for the priest. He intended to tell Michalak to cool it later.

As the Martinis were leaving, Father Martini said, "Isabella will ask Roberto, my brother in *La Farmacia,* for something for your pain tomorrow, Sergeant. Supplies are almost exhausted but perhaps he can prepare something for you."

"That would help a lot, Father! Thank you, Isabella."

Isabella gave Michalak a wide smile and Rugby thought that she looked thrilled at the chance to return. She seemed to float up the basement steps.

May 10, 1944

6:00 AM

The next morning Rugby climbed the bell tower and strung an antenna. He logged military traffic. Later, Michalak, as Rugby cranked the hand-powered generator, keyed an encrypted dispatch including their location.

Fifth Army Headquarters was dismayed to learn American rangers were hiding in the church of a town targeted for a massive bombing campaign. The report of the soldiers' location went up the chain of command to Lieutenant General Mark Clark. The general already was uneasy about the negative publicity and international criticism from the bombing of the old Benedictine abbey. Furthermore, Clark considered bombing friendly forces repugnant. He ordered the targeting of Alvito stayed until he checked with his theater commander.

Although food was in short supply in Alvito, Isabella brought a bewildering array of provisions to the soldiers. Michalak's ankle was in poor condition but he managed to hobble around with a crutch. As the days passed, he and Isabella spent increasing amounts of time together, usually in the shadows of the cellar, where large casks of wine made from spicy local grapes, known as *Cesanese*, were stored.

The rangers continued their program of reporting. For two weeks they broadcast at random times and intervals, changed frequencies routinely, and never transmitted more than a few minutes.

May 24, 1944

9:00 AM

Over the past week an SS direction finding station in Rome, searching for OSS transmissions, had detected several broadcasts on known enemy frequencies. Additional bearings taken from Florence triangulated a transmitter in the vicinity of Alvito. After a series of discussions between the intelligence officer of *XIV Panzer Korps*, Field Marshall Kesselring's staff, the Gestapo, and the SS Command in Italy, *Herr Oberst* Hermann Küchler received a call on his field telephone from an SS officer.

"Küchler? SS *Obergruppenführer* Lohse, in Rome. What's going on in Alvito?"

"What do you mean?" asked Küchler. "The road is open and supplies are flowing to the front. If there's a problem, it's not here. In fact, I'm surprised they haven't bombed us yet."

"Yes, General von Senger noticed that too." Ominously, added Lohse, "So did Kesselring."

"It's luck, I guess. I still expect them to bomb us—and soon! The Allies took Monte Cassino; I understand they broke out of the Anzio beachhead yesterday."

"*Das ist korrekt*," said Lohse. "They're also mounting an air assault on the *Adolph Hitler* Line, which the *Führer* has renamed the *Dora* Line."

Küchler snorted at the hypocrisy. "But that could destroy the right flank. I could be under attack from three directions!"

"Retreat would be ill advised. You know what happens to deserters. We have several detachments of SS roaming behind the lines looking for the cowards. Your job is to stand and die for the *Vaterland*."

Küchler rolled his eyes and waited.

"However," said Lohse after an awkward silence, "that's not the reason I called. We've noticed enemy radio traffic coming from your vicinity. What do you know about that?"

"*Nichts*! I'll have to look into it."

"Precisely! And to help you along, I've sent you a mobile DF van. SS *Sturmbannführer* Nassler will be there soon. A good man. You can thank me later, perhaps. Now do your job. I suggest you burn your files."

May 24, 1944

2:00 PM

Father Martini was having a Spartan meal with Küchler. Bread, wine and a small cheese were all the café could offer. The townspeople were hoarding the other foodstuffs.

The *Oberst* had been silent for some time and Father Martini could tell he was tense.

"Eugenio, has anything unusual been happening in town? Have you seen any strangers?"

"What do you mean? I've noticed that the siren has been silent, of course, but nothing else." Martini thought his lie might be a sin. He felt guilty for betraying his friend, but Alvito was more important. And besides, his sister was in love with the young sergeant.

"Listen carefully, Father, the SS are coming to town. They're curious about some radio traffic. If you know anything, for both our sakes, you have to tell me now. They could exterminate every person in town! They've done it before."

Father Martini, troubled, looked away. But he knew that Küchler's suspicions were aroused.

"Father, please, if anyone in this town is working for the Allies, I need to know." Küchler stared directly into Father Martini's eyes.

"No, I know nothing." The priest averted his eyes and focused on the old church. "Hopefully San Valerio will give you an excuse to surrender soon. There are rumors the Allies are almost here."

"The SS are not keen on surrender. Be very careful. If you're lying to me, we're both in trouble."

"Enjoy your lunch, Hermann. I will pray for our deliverance."

Küchler shook his head, threw some coins on the table, and stormed away.

May 24, 1944

3:30 PM

After the meal, Father Martini went directly to the church cellar. Though torn between betrayal and the stigma of spying, he'd resolved to warn Captain Rugby about the SS. Maybe the Americans would stop broadcasting. "Captain, I just spoke with the *Oberst*. Although I don't like to spy for either side, I must tell you that the SS are coming. They know about your radio."

"Damn," said Rugby. "They picked up our general location. Well, the best I can do is stop broadcasting today. The battle is in its final throes; our messages might save lives. I need to get back on the air tomorrow."

"Where are the Allies now?"

"They're close; they could be here in an hour or a week. Who knows? Ask San Valerio."

"It would be a tragedy if anyone dies with liberation so near. I'm sure the saint will protect all of us, including the *Oberst*."

"I hope you're right, Father."

May 24, 1944

8:00 PM

Küchler was tense the rest of the day. He was in his office that evening when *Korporal* Wandt saw Isabella carrying a basket of vegetables, wine and a small chunk of Mortadella sausage, enter the church. When she left with an empty basket a few moments later, he reported to Küchler.

"She took food into the church and left it there?"

"*Jawohl, Herr Oberst.*"

"*Gott verdampft.* They're feeding someone in there and hiding it from me. I'm going to deal with that priest now!"

Thirty minutes later, Küchler found Father Martini in his church by the Communion railing. He confronted the priest and demanded to know who the food was for. "Don't tell me that food was for you, Father. I've had enough of your lies. I thought we were friends."

"Hermann, we are friends."

"It's *Herr Oberst,* Father. What's going on in the church?"

"I was praying to San Valerio that it would all be resolved by the arrival of the Allies."

"I demand that you explain yourself."

"Please, No fighting. I'll make an introduction, if you agree to come alone, and unarmed."

"Alone? Unarmed? You want me to trust you now?" Küchler shook his head in disgust.

"I beg you," said Father Martini. "I give you my word, in the name of the Holy Virgin, that it will be safe."

To Küchler, the priest seemed quite distraught—and those pledges to the Virgin were usually sincere. Frustrated and angry, he wondered what to do. Should he assemble a raiding party? Go in without backup? Fortunately, *Korporal* Wandt knew where he had gone—if he didn't return the men would know to follow. He stared at the priest for some time, and, finally, decided to meet him halfway.

"Okay, Father, I'm willing to come alone—but armed." Küchler pulled his Walther P-38 sidearm out. "Let's go—you first."

Father Martini led the way down the steps to the cellar. When Küchler reached the bottom step he saw an American officer. Küchler pointed his weapon at the man and the American raised his hands.

"*Was ist los? Einer Amerikaner?*" asked Küchler.

"*Jawohl, Herr Oberst,* Captain Carl Rugby, U.S. Army Rangers."

"*Sie sprechen Deutsch?*"

"*Ja, aber möchte Ich lieber Englisch,*" answered Rugby.

"Okay, *Englisch geht.* What are you doing here? Do you have a radio?" Küchler was nervous and wanted answers.

"C'mon, *Herr Oberst,* that's a full colonel in the *Wehrmacht,* right? I can salute you, but I can't tell you what I'm doing." Rugby snapped to attention and saluted Küchler.

"Very well, you're under arrest."

"Please *Herr Oberst,* don't do this," pleaded the priest

Küchler returned the salute. "Father, I cannot have enemy agents in my town. At least he's still in uniform, although I doubt that will make much difference to the SS. I regret that, but I have no choice. Captain, you're my prisoner."

"I don't think so," said Michalak, hopping from behind some wine casks, into the light. He was armed with a rifle pointed directly at Küchler. Isabella, who'd returned earlier, with a small container of olive oil and bread, followed the sergeant with a terrified look on her face.

"So, Father, there are more than one, eh? What else haven't you told me?" He gave the priest a disappointed look.

"I guess we have a Mexican standoff here," said Rugby, with his hands still raised.

"I don't know what that means," said Küchler, "but I have a company of men who know where I am."

"Uh-huh," said Michalak. "Tell me *Oberst*, sir, have you noticed Alvito has not been bombed? Can you figure out why? Well, maybe it's because of us. If we don't keep reporting in, you can kiss your ass goodbye. Maybe you want to chew on that?"

Küchler thought for a moment. His hopes for survival of the war receded as he considered his position—squeezed between the SS and the American rangers. He was at a disadvantage and would likely die in any firefight. His troops would undoubtedly kill the Americans and the priest and his sister but that was little consolation. And, when the SS troops arrived they might slaughter the rest of the people in town. Even if he survived a shootout the bombings would be devastating. He needed time to think so he slowly lowered his weapon, followed by Michalak.

"*Herr Oberst*," said the priest, "please don't do anything that will endanger the town."

"Father, these Americans are endangering your town. What were you thinking when you allowed them to hide in your church?"

Rugby said, "*Herr Oberst*, don't blame the priest. Sanctuary is a tradition in the Church. But why do we have to fight? *Vielleicht Man soll die schlafenden Löwen nicht wecken.* May I propose a truce?"

"I don't know. I should kill you, but yes, it would be prudent to let sleeping dogs lie. We can suspend hostilities—for now." He holstered his pistol and Michalak propped his rifle against a wine cask.

"*Herr Oberst*," said Rugby, "We need to talk about the military situation. What's your name?"

Father Martini introduced Küchler who nodded and suggested that he and the captain sit at the table. Michalak hovered near his rifle.

"The military situation?" asked Küchler. "Men are dying like flies on both sides; why should it be different for us?"

"Look Küchler, the most dangerous time in war is at the beginning and end of combat operations. We both know the battle for Rome is almost over. If you play your cards right, you and your men can survive."

"Captain, I'm listening but I must admit that survival seems remote."

"Do you play chess? Maybe the good Father could find us a set, and Isabella might fetch us some wine?"

Father Martini rushed upstairs and returned with a chess set. Isabella poured some wine. Küchler noticed that she smiled at him for the first time; perhaps she was having second thoughts about him.

"I should tell you *Herr Oberst*," commented Rugby wryly, "that I was chess champion in my Boy Scout troop." He opened the game with queen's pawn.

"Really, Captain? I was champion of the *Bayrisches Schachjugend*, the Bavarian Youth Chess Club." He smiled at Rugby's aggressive opening and, on his second move, accepted Rugby's queen's gambit.

After several more moves, Rugby moved his queen onto the board.

"Captain," Küchler said graciously, "It's dangerous to move an unprotected queen onto contested territory,"

"Dangerous? But that's what rangers do."

Küchler smiled and advanced a bishop. "So what are we going to do, Captain? The SS will kill us both if I don't close you down."

"I can understand that. Still, I'm sure you don't want to be bombed and your war will be over any day now." Rugby countered with a knight.

"True. When will your forces arrive?" asked Küchler as he took a pawn.

"Unless you wish to die fighting, or become POWs, you and your men should leave now. We've been told your defenses are collapsing—even the *Adolph Hitler* Line is crumbling."

"Ha! It's the *Dora* Line now. Our propaganda minister, Goebbels, is earning his keep." Küchler snapped up another pawn.

"We have propaganda, too. In any event, I expect relief within hours, or a day or so. Of course, the timing also depends on your people. You mentioned the SS. Are they coming here? When? How many?"

"Enough to find your radio, arrest me for treason, and murder everyone in town."

"You could surrender the town to me." Rugby frowned at his board position.

Küchler placed his queen next to Rugby's king. "I don't think so, but let me think about my options tonight. I must consider my men. Meanwhile, checkmate!" He looked over at the priest, Isabella and Michalak, and nodded. "Good night, Father. *Signorina*. You too, Sergeant. Thank you for not shooting me."

"Are you coming back with your men, *Herr Oberst*?" asked Michalak.

"Sergeant, Sun Tzu said, 'All warfare is based on deception.' If I say no, will you believe me?"

"I will," said Rugby.

"Thank you Captain. For the moment I shall honor our cease-fire."

As Küchler walked back to City Hall, he decided he would not bring *Korporal* Wandt into his confidence about the Americans—at least not before he decided what to do about his troops. The *Korporal* was loyal to his commander but, with the SS due to arrive soon, that information was dangerous and it could place Wandt in a compromised position. Küchler told Wandt that food was being stockpiled in the event of prolonged combat when the Allies arrived.

May 25, 1944

10:00 AM

Küchler had spent a restless night when *Sturmbannführer* Jens Nassler's staff car, followed by his direction finding van, rolled into Alvito. Nassler was a former *Hitlerjugend* member and Nazi party loyalist. He'd been hunting partisans and OSS agents. Using the van, and a detector on his staff car, his team could locate a transmitter in under an hour. With two bearings, and a known distance between the two detectors, it was a simple calculation to fix the location of the target. Nassler's orders were to shut down any hostile transmitters.

The *Sturmbannführer* strode into Küchler's headquarters in City Hall and demanded an immediate audience with the *Oberst*. Küchler, who'd dreaded the meeting, invited Nassler into his office.

"Welcome, *Sturmbannführer*. Congratulations. You've beaten the Allies to Alvito."

"*Herr Oberst*," said Nassler, oblivious to the sarcasm, "the Allies will never breach our lines. I'm confident in the *Führer*, and I look forward to serving him by tracking and destroying the enemy radio."

"Good for you, Nassler," said Küchler. "I'm not sure which lines you refer to, but I, too, wish to serve Germany. Is there anything you need from me to start work?"

"Yes, I need to consult with your men who control the electricity. We may need to turn off power, block by block, as we search for the enemy's radio."

"Of course. But Alvito is a small town; I'm not certain there is more than one transformer. In fact, there aren't too many blocks. But, please, be my guest. *Korporal* Wandt will make the necessary introductions."

"Thank you, *Herr Oberst. Sieg Heil!*"

Küchler made a half-hearted arm gesture. Nassler smirked, turned on his heels, and left.

That afternoon Nassler sent the DF van to the east and climbed into his vehicle. When he turned on his detector and tuned it to an enemy frequency, he picked up a brief signal. However, by the time the van was prepared to track, the transmitter was silent. He cursed his lost opportunity.

May 25, 1944

3:00 PM

Küchler, supervising the destruction of his unit's records, heard the sound of mortar and small arms fire. Allied forces skirmished within sight of Alvito. He retrieved his field glasses and headed for the bell tower. When he climbed the steps he discovered Captain Rugby was there already, watching the battle through his glasses.

"So, Captain," said Küchler, "it's a matter of hours, is it?"

"Yes, *Herr Oberst*. I see the SS are here too. You didn't tell them about us?"

"No. My war is over. The SS officer is a fanatic named Nassler. The fool thinks the Allies have lost the war."

"Are you certain you don't want to surrender?" asked Rugby. "How about your men?"

"I've decided to release them. They are free to choose their own fate; retreat if possible, surrender, or fight. I suspect most will wish to withdraw to fight again, after all these are *Wehrmacht* soldiers. Sadly, retreat is perilous with the SS slaughtering any troops they find without orders. Some of the men, undoubtedly, will choose surrender."

"Alright, *Herr Oberst*. Those who surrender will be treated honorably by me. And what will you do?"

"I think tonight I shall consider my options; surrender, death by hanging, death by firing squad, or a painful death. Perhaps I'll cheat the hangman and take cyanide. I probably can get some from that SS idiot."

Rugby smiled at the Oberst's cynicism. "Please don't do anything rash. We still can survive this madness. *Alles ist noch möglich.*"

"Still possible?" asked Küchler. "Perhaps. But you must be careful, Captain. If Nassler finds you, he'll kill you in a heartbeat. He already has a single DF bearing on you. In fact, I still should kill you. However, I fail to see what that would accomplish, and your sergeant is probably covering the stairs. Our truce continues. *Tschuss.*"

May 26, 1944

10:00 AM

As battle raged on the outskirts of town, Nassler's men triangulated Rugby's transmitter in the church. Nassler rushed into Küchler's office to demand he organize an *Aktion,* including reprisals, but he found only *Korporal* Wandt.

"I think you'll find him at the church. He's with the priest. They're discussing what will happen when the Allies arrive. We've received no further orders and some of the men have left."

"Some of your men have deserted? You *Wehrmacht* men are cowards!"

"They retreat so that they may return to battle," said Wandt, giving Nassler a hostile look. "And I'm still here. Someone must protect the *Oberst.*"

"No one can protect him from me if he's planning to surrender!"

When Nassler arrived at the church, he stationed his driver and the other two storm troopers from the van inside the entrance.

Nassler wandered the first floor. He observed the ceiling trimmed with gold; he fumed that it hadn't been sent to Germany. He became angrier when he saw valuable art, including a crucifixion in the Sacristy by Cavalier d'Arpino, and a wooden statue of *La Madonna di Loreto* sculpted by Giovanni Stolz. Determined to find both the transmitter and Küchler, Nassler eventually discovered the steps to the cellar. Descending, he heard people talking and recognized Küchler's voice. He cocked his *Schmeisser* MP 40 machine pistol and charged down.

At the bottom he was startled to discover a priest, Küchler, and an American officer, seated around a table. Confronting them, he shouted, "Küchler, you're a traitor. I'm going to kill you!"

"Go ahead, Nassler. I'm all yours." Küchler stood and turned to block Nassler's line of fire and to protect the priest.

Father Martini said, "Wait—" but he was interrupted by Michalak who roared out of the shadows, firing at the same time. His bullets riddled Nassler, but Nassler's MP 40 fired several stray rounds that flashed around the cellar, striking wine casks and ricocheting off the stone walls. One slug hit Rugby in the chest. He fell at Küchler's feet, bleeding profusely.

For a few moments everyone froze in position; the room filled with the smell of cordite and smoke from the weapons. Shaken, Küchler looked down at Rugby. Wine from a ruptured cask spread on the stone floor and mixed with Rugby's blood. Isabella shrieked and ran to Rugby. But the captain was beyond help. Kneeling in Rugby's blood and the wine, Isabella began to weep while she rocked his body back and forth.

At that instant, intense gunfire erupted in the church upstairs. Sneaking up the steps, Father Martini saw the bodies of Nassler's three storm troopers sprawled on the floor. British soldiers were spreading throughout the church. The priest raised his hands and shouted, "Over here! *Benvenuto a Alvito.* God knows we need you."

Several soldiers dashed over and patted him down while a British non-commissioned officer strode up.

"Father, I'm Colour Sergeant William Lawrence, British XIII Corps Combat Assault Team. The Germans are in full flight. My orders are to secure this church and determine the status of two American soldiers who were hiding here."

"I'm afraid the American captain just died. His sergeant is alive, down in the cellar. He's injured, but he'll be fine."

As Lawrence turned to go down the steps, Father Martini said, "Wait, Sergeant. There's a German *Oberst* down there, too, and a dead SS Officer. My sister is also there. Please hold your fire. I'm sure the *Oberst* is peaceful."

"Okay, Father," said Lawrence. "Let's both go. Since you're so certain, you can go first."

Both men smelled cordite as they went down the steps. Father Martini stepped over the body of the dead SS officer and Lawrence stopped, with his weapon ready. Michalak leaned against a wine cask holding his rifle.

"Who are you, mate?"

"Sergeant Ray Michalak, U.S. Army Rangers."

Lawrence continued to the bottom of the steps. An *Oberst* sat at the table, and a young woman, her dress drenched in blood and wine, was crying and holding a dead U.S. Army captain. The priest had gone directly to the girl, whom he was trying to comfort. Lawrence stepped over the dead SS officer.

"Sergeant Michalak," said Lawrence, "Who's the German?"

"Excuse me," said Küchler. "I'm *Oberst* Hermann Küchler, *XIV Panzer Korps.*"

"Thank you, *Oberst*," said Lawrence. "And who is the dead SS officer?"

"That was SS Sturmbannführer Nassler," said Küchler. "He brought a direction finding team to town and I have a company of soldiers. However, I've released them from their duties; I suspect many of them have melted away."

"Yes *Oberst,* but not all of them. We took quite a few prisoners—and that includes you."

"Perhaps not," said Küchler. "I've already surrendered to Sergeant Michalak."

"That's right," said Michalak. "He's my prisoner."

"And the girl?"

"She's my sister," said Father Martini. "This is Isabella."

"Well Sergeant," said Lawrence, "this *Oberst* may have important information and he speaks English. He's quite a valuable catch. I need to deliver him to an Intelligence officer."

"No!" said Isabella. "He stays here; he's a prisoner of the Americans. I will not have him lost in the confusion of battle. Along with this poor American captain and Sergeant Michalak, he saved this town."

All the men smiled at the firmness in her voice and her innocence about the realities of war.

"Can't your Intelligence officer come here to interrogate the *Oberst*?" pleaded Father Martini. "Please. Let him stay here until the front lines stabilize."

"Well, it's rather irregular, but I'll refer the issue to my lieutenant. I do think, though, that it might be a rather jolly idea, Sergeant Michalak, to relieve your prisoner of his weapon."

Küchler grinned ruefully and handed his Walther pistol, butt first, to Sergeant Michalak.

Lawrence saluted the *Oberst*. "Thank you, sir, for surrendering your weapon. And Sergeant, I will send you a medical corpsman to look after that ankle."

"Can you arrange to remove the dead SS Officer?" asked the priest.

"Of course. We'll also collect the captain's body."

"No thank you," said Father Martini. "Captain Rugby should stay here. I will give him the last rites. We'll take care of the arrangements."

"Alright Father, I'll notify Fifth Army and Sergeant Michalak should take one of the captain's dog tags."

August 14, 1969

10:30 AM

Father Eugenio Martini hummed with excitement; For hundreds of years, August 14th had been the date dedicated to San Valerio. Over the last twenty-five years, the citizens of Alvito also celebrated the *Miracle* on the same day. As a bonus, the town commemorated the twenty-fifth anniversary, albeit a few months late, of its liberation from German occupation—May 26, 1944.

The priest's hair had thinned and turned gray and his waistline had expanded over the years. He was in Landini's Dry Cleaners inspecting the annual cleaning of the World War II relics. The relics were symbolic evidence of the *Miracle.* They normally had a place of honor in *La Chiesa del Miracolo* (The Church of the Miracle), formerly *La Parrocchiale di San Simeone.* Since the end of the war the relics had been displayed in an annual pageant that honored San Valerio. The parade began with a procession that left the church, crossed Piazza Marconi, marched up Corso Silvio Castrucci, and then turned and proceeded up the hill to the *Castello.* The castle was decked out with decorations and rows of tables, enormous casks of wine, kegs of beer, and panoply of food. Hundreds of visitors were expected.

"Father," asked Landini, "are the uniforms to your liking?"

"Yes, thank you," said the priest. "Please mount them on these poles. They'll follow our statue of *La Madonna di Loreto* in the procession."

"There's talk in town that we'll have some important visitors," said Baglio. "Is that true, Father?" Baglio, who owned the butcher shop next door to Landini's, had been pressed into service to help mount the uniforms.

"Yes, I'm expecting *Herr Oberst* Küchler—well, I guess he's not a colonel anymore—and my sister and her husband."

"So the American is coming too?" asked Landini. "That will be nice, Father—a very special celebration."

"Yes, a wonderful reminder of our *Miracle* and the grace of San Valerio. That is why the uniforms must be perfect."

"But Father," said Landini, "you know I can't do anything about the blood and wine stains on the captain's uniform."

"Of course," said the priest. "It was God's will and the people will understand."

●●●

A tall, distinguished looking man in his early sixties, dressed formally in a blue suit and tie, stood next to the old café in Piazza Marconi. *Herr Professor* Herman Küchler, formerly *Herr Oberst* Küchler, commander of the German garrison in Alvito during the war, was waiting patiently for the procession to begin.

The band had assembled and the piazza was crowded with residents and visitors. With a beat of the drums the procession started out from the church led by Father Martini and his brother Roberto, the mayor. The statue of the Madonna, a priceless carving, was next, followed by the uniforms, the band, town notables and sisters from the *Convento*, the choir, provincial and national flag bearers, and others, including a few of the town's mangy dogs. Following the time-beaten path, the Martinis led the procession onto Piazza Marconi.

Halfway across the piazza, with the crowd cheering, the German waved at the priest. Father Martini saw the gesture, grinned, whispered in his brother's ear, and broke out of the procession—which halted and milled about in confusion.

"*Herr* Küchler," said the Father, "*Benvenuto*. It's so good to see you again."

"Father, you old devil, it's a special treat for me too. And please, call me Hermann. Remember? Will the others be here?"

"Yes, of course, Hermann. They said they were coming after I told them you would be here. I'm expecting Isabella and Ray."

"Is your sister still as beautiful as ever?" asked Küchler.

"See for yourself. There they are. We'll talk later."

The priest returned to his position and the band burst into a cacophony of noise. The procession, in disarray, reformed in a different order, and resumed its march.

Küchler turned and smiled a welcome to a handsome couple who wove their way through the crowd. The woman, about forty, was ravishing and the man, tall and tanned, walked with a limp.

"*Herr Oberst*," said the woman. She wrapped her arms around Küchler.

"*Gruss Gott*," he said, embarrassed. "Isabella, my God, you're getting more beautiful with age. And, please, I'm not an *Oberst* anymore."

So, Hermann, *wie geht's?*" asked Isabella's husband, Ray Michalak. "You look good. How's your chess game?"

Hermann Küchler smiled again. "You look good as well."

The three friends sat down at the café on the edge of Piazza Marconi. Isabella ordered a carafe of water. The men ordered beer.

"They're calling it a *Miracle*, you know—the fact that Alvito was never bombed," said Küchler.

"I think it was," said Isabella. "During the battle for Cassino it felt as though the bombs were walking towards us. With you and your troops stationed in town, we were convinced the allies would target the town. And then Ray and Captain Rugby arrived."

Küchler nodded. "My superiors also wondered why we were never bombed. Then they sent that lunatic, Nassler to look for Ray's radio."

Isabella smiled. "The townspeople believe they were saved by two soldiers—Captain Rugby and Ray, who hid in the church. They were soldiers like San Valerio. The people believe the saint sent the Americans."

Küchler looked up at the old church bell tower where the antenna had been strung. "I don't know about the saint, but I owe them my life."

"Hermann," asked Ray, "what happened to you after the war?"

"I was interrogated by the British several times and I stayed here until Rome was liberated. I was then sent to the Modena Allied POW camp. I was released in late 1945 and returned to Bavaria. I live in Ulm now."

"Was it difficult in the POW camp?"

"I was grateful to be alive. And you? Couldn't they fix that ankle?"

"It was beat up pretty good. But after we buried the captain the Brits got me to an American hospital ship in the port of Naples, the *USS Ernest Hands*. They had to re-break the ankle, and then put on a cast. They jerked around with it several times. It finally healed, but I've always had a limp. The boat disembarked us in England so that it could take on casualties from Normandy. I got back to the states in the spring of 1945. In 1946 I went back to Alvito and married Isabella."

"What say we take a walk?" said Küchler. "We can stop at the cemetery, visit Captain Rugby, and then join Isabella's brothers at the festival."

As they crossed Piazza Marconi they were startled by the beep of a horn. An old black Fiat sped across the piazza. Father Martini climbed out of the passenger seat, waved at the driver, and handed a bouquet of carnations and chrysanthemums to Isabella. "I thought you might be visiting the cemetery. I think the captain would appreciate these."

Isabella smiled as the old friends gathered around the grave of Captain Carl Rugby, U.S. Army Rangers. It was a beautiful day.

Illegals

Getting into America isn't easy. The Americans have naval forces patrolling their waters to prevent those of us from Cuba, as well as elsewhere, from reaching their shores. When I joined the others assembled at the docks in Havana I knew it would be a complicated journey. I never dreamt that I would find myself involved in a criminal case brought by the United States government.

Smugglers bundled us into groups according to our family names and packed us in large shipping containers. We received just enough water to keep our throats from getting too dry. The children were scared when they were separated from us, but at least they were with their brothers and sisters, again sorted by name.

Our destination was San Francisco. That meant we had to travel through the Panama Canal. During the journey, time blurred and the air became stale. We worried about the children but we could hear them singing songs to keep themselves occupied. Fortunately the weather was cool for Central America, so it didn't get too hot in the containers.

When we arrived at Pier 13 in San Francisco, they continued to segregate us. First, they took the children away. We could sense their bewilderment and hear their shouts of desperation when they realized they would never see us again. But what could we do? We were still trapped in the containers.

A few hours later they came for us. They took away our clothes and gave us flimsy wraps from Sumatra. My sister and other family members went in one batch. I went in another. My batch was trucked to a shop called Sandy's House of Pleasures on Battery Street.

Many customers looked me over. The man who finally purchased me only did so after first admiring me from many angles. He appreciated my figure. I wasn't too tall or too short or even too fat. Apparently he liked me even without decent clothing. I guessed that he would fool around with me in front of his friends, who would all admire him and be jealous.

Can you imagine my surprise when we left the shop and a flock of federal agents swooped down and arrested us? They dragged us to the lockup in the old federal building on Golden Gate Avenue.

The man was booked, fingerprinted, and told he could make one phone call. I was carried off to another room where an assistant United States attorney looked me over. "You'll be the jewel in the crown in my case against that man and the shop that sold you," she said. "Trafficking in illegals is the charge! It's an open and shut case." Of course, as an illegal, they detained me. I can tell you horror tales about the federal prison system. People lusted after me all the time. I prayed to Saint Salvador daily under the sneering faces of the guards.

I later discovered that the man who had purchased me was a San Francisco lawyer from the firm of Gurth and Gurth, in the Russ Building, on Montgomery Street. His name was Jack Boone and he was an immigration lawyer. He was representing himself in this case. Sandy's House of Pleasures was represented by Gurth and Gurth.

After several months, the case went to trial in the U.S. District Court for Northern California. A senior judge named Giuseppe Zirpoli, who was close to retirement, presided. The trial had been underway for several days, and was in recess when I was brought into the courtroom by a federal marshal. It looked like the media had latched onto the case; the room was packed to overflowing with reporters, onlookers, other attorneys, a law class from some university, and a camera crew.

At the end of the recess, the judge returned to the courtroom. I trembled when I saw him; he was one of the men who had examined me at the shop! Nevertheless, I maintained a discreet silence.

Judge Zirpoli called the courtroom to order and the assistant U.S. attorney moved toward her peroration.

"Your Honor," she said with confidence, "the government has presented evidence that Sandy's House of Pleasure**s**, on Battery Street, has trafficked in illegals. Despite some of the counterfeit packaging, which alleges the illegals are from Sumatra, we have DNA tests that prove conclusively they are from Cuba. They are, in fact, the legendary Cohiba Robustos!"

Yes, I am—and proud of it, I thought. However, she wasn't done yet.

She cited her authorities. "As you know, President Kennedy signed an executive order directing the Federal Trade Commission and the United States Customs Service to prohibit the importation and sale of illegals. Sandy's House of Pleasures sold, and Mr. Boone is guilty of purchasing, such prohibited merchandise! He was arrested with the contraband still in his possession." She closed with a Latin expression, "*Res ipsa loquitor*, Your Honor, it speaks for itself."

Judge Zirpoli nodded, although I could tell from the way he rolled his eyes, that he had little enthusiasm for the case. He stared at me for a while, before asking, "What do you say, Mr. Boone, to that comment by the government? The U.S. attorney seems to think she has an easy conviction."

I wondered how Mr. Boone would slither out of the charge. I waited breathlessly for his reply, hoping that I wouldn't have to testify.

"Your Honor," said he, "it's true that the importation and sale of Cuban cigars has been prohibited by an executive order for over forty years. However, according to the 1980 Refugee Act, Title 8, United States Code, section 1101, any Cuban nationals that leave Cuba legally, and who land successfully on American soil, are automatically granted permanent residence and asylum in the United States. Even if they leave Cuba *illegally*—and that has by no means been demonstrated by the government—they are granted the right to apply for asylum. In neither case are they detained. *This cigar* is a Cuban national. The government has certified that fact with DNA tests. This Cohiba Robusto clearly has satisfied either, one, the statutory requirement for automatic asylum, or, two, has qualified for permission to apply for asylum, and, hence, by definition, is legal. The government had no right to detain this cigar. That's black letter law, Judge. I submit that federal law, approved by Congress, holds sway over a presidential executive order. Further, in any clash between the powers of the president and the powers of the Congress, it is long-standing precedent that the courts resolve the conflict by casting the deciding vote. I move, therefore, for an immediate dismissal of all charges against myself and Sandy's House of Pleasures."

The assistant U.S. attorney's face turned red with rage. She rose with clenched fists to sputter an argument against this clever manipulation of legal intent. "Your Honor, I object—"

Judge Zirpoli smiled wryly. "Please, Madame Prosecutor, keep your seat. Motion denied! Mr. Boone's argument is quite persuasive to me."

At that, a lawyer from Gurth and Gurth jumped up. "Your Honor, we agree with you. We've prepared this brief in support of that motion." He waved a seven-inch-thick document over his head.

Judge Zirpoli recoiled at the sight of the large document. "You can keep your supporting brief; I've decided the case. But, perhaps in the future, and in the interests of judicial efficiency, your briefs will be . . . brief."

The judge then dismissed the case with prejudice—on the spot. He invited Mr. Boone to join him in his chambers and adjourned the courtroom. Reporters jammed the entrance to the courtroom as they raced out, intent upon scooping their rivals with news of this startling ruling—which, in effect, legalized Cuban cigars in the Northern District of California. No one in the courtroom expected the government to appeal. The United States Ninth Circuit Court of Appeals, also headquartered in liberal San Francisco, was unlikely to reverse the decision. A lost appeal, in effect, would be costly to the government since it would legalize Cuban cigars in the nine western states that composed the Ninth Circuit.

In the judge's chambers, the federal marshals returned me to Mr. Boone. As I wondered what would happen next, I was dismayed to see the judge produce another cigar from inside his gown. It was my sister! That was just before he pulled out a cigar cutter and a book of matches. Help!

Baggage

Ed Axelrod, an attorney, was traveling from Washington DC to Toledo, Ohio, for an important meeting, when it happened. He first flew National Airlines, from Reagan Washington Airport to Cleveland. Then Ed connected to National Express, for the short flight to Toledo. This required changing planes as well as carriers, although National Express was a subsidiary of National Airlines. Ed worried his luggage might miss the connection so he first checked his bags to Cleveland. Then he fetched them in Cleveland and rechecked them, at the National Express desk, to Toledo.

"Are you sure the bags will make the flight?" Ed was anxious when he asked the clerk. The bags contained critical depositions from his firm's big legal case.

"Oh, yes, Mr. Axelrod. No problem. Here are your boarding pass and baggage checks. You leave from Gate Two."

Ed passed through security and went to his gate. His airplane, a Brazilian Embraer 130 commuter with eighty-five seats, was ready for boarding. Ed wondered where the rest of the passengers were. *Maybe they're already on-board or this is an interim stop, and I'm the only passenger boarding.* But when he stepped into the cabin Ed saw he was the only passenger.

An attractive flight attendant stood inside the door.

"Mr. Axelrod? Hi. I'm Cindy, your flight attendant. You're our only passenger today. The captain asked me to seat you in 21C, to balance the load; if you don't mind."

"Did my bags make it?"

"I'm sure that's no problem, Mr. Axelrod. Relax, enjoy your flight. Would you like a drink before takeoff?"

Ed smiled and accepted a drink. He'd noticed the sink in the galley had several empty miniature bottles of gin. He hoped it wasn't the pilot who'd been nipping.

●●●

At Toledo's Express Airport ten miles west of the city, the National Express gate agent, Betty Marx, was on the phone with her supervisor, Phil, in Newark.

"Look, Phil! Damn it. Cindy said she personally sat this guy in 21C. But, when they landed, he wasn't on the plane. She said the pilot had reported radio problems; apparently lots of sunspot activity. Landing was delayed an hour. All the seats in row twenty-one—both sides of the aisle—were slightly scorched, too."

"Did the passenger's bags arrive?"

"Two bags arrived. That's what so strange; usually we misplace a bag, especially when there are only a few passengers on board; but we're not used to misplacing passengers."

"Cindy must be into the sauce again. Send the bags to Lost Luggage in Denver."

"What if someone asks about the passenger?"

"Well, he wasn't on the plane," declared Phil. "I assume he never made the connection. They must've screwed up in Cleveland and keyed in his boarding pass, as though he boarded. Go into the computer and correct the record."

"Okay, I got to run; I have to turnaround the Cincinnati flight."

● ● ●

Ed Axelrod was shaky. He'd just awakened and he was sweating profusely; the air was unusually humid. *Why is it so bloody hot?* Ed was sitting in an airport and bags were sliding down a chute, onto a rotating carousel. The building was not enclosed and a tropical breeze surged through the baggage area. *Where the hell am I? This sure don't look like Toledo to me.* Ed stood and walked over to the carousel. He looked at the tags on the bags dropping onto the carousel, Destination Airport: GUM. *Where the hell is GUM?*

"Excuse me sir, can I help you?" Ed looked up and saw a man with a jacket sporting an Air Pacific emblem. "You seem lost."

"Where am I? I was flying to Toledo."

"Toledo? This, sir, is Guam. We get bags sent to Toledo. You're the first passenger."

Guam? What the hell am I doing in Guam?

"What about my bags?"

"They probably went to Toledo."

"Is there a courtesy phone to Air Pacific?"

Ed strode to the wall and picked up a courtesy telephone.

● ● ●

"Good afternoon. This is Air Pacific. My name's John, may I help you?

"You bet, John, I seem to be in the wrong airport and my luggage went astray, too. There are critical papers in—"

"Did you say the wrong airport? Air Pacific delivered you to the wrong airport?"

Ed explained that he last remembered boarding a National Express plane in Cleveland and now he was in Guam.

"Sir, that's ridiculous. If you really flew on National, please call them and stop playing jokes. If you keep this up I will report you to the TSA!"

"But—" The Air Pacific agent hung up.

Ed dialed an 800 number for National. He was worried about making his breakfast meeting the next morning in Toledo. *And where were those bags?*

"Good morning, this is National Airlines. My name is Josephine. May I help you?"

"Yes, it seems you flew me to the wrong airport. I have to get to Toledo immediately."

"Please, sir. With the way airport security is these days; it's simply not possible to get on the wrong airplane. Did your baggage go to the wrong airport too?"

"I don't know where my bags are. There are very important documents in them. But I'm in Guam now."

"Well, we fly to Guam but our flight doesn't leave from Los Angeles International for two hours. What are your ticket and baggage check numbers?"

Ed read the numbers off his boarding pass and his baggage tags to the agent.

"Well, according to the computer . . . excuse me . . . you're Mr. Axelrod?"

"That's right, Ed Axelrod."

"Well, according to the computer, you never made the flight from Cleveland to Toledo."

"But I checked my bags in Cleveland."

"Yes, and Toledo reported that your two bags arrived. Since they were unclaimed, we shipped them to our Lost Luggage depot in Denver. But you never boarded the plane."

This is nuts. "But, damn it, I'm in Guam! How'd I get here?"

"I can't help you, Mr. Axelrod. Would you like to speak with my supervisor?"

"You bet your sweet ass I would."

"Now, now, Mr. Axelrod. There's no cause to be rude. I'll transfer you."

● ● ●

"This is Laurie, reservations supervisor. May I help you?"

"Laurie, you people have flown me to Guam when I wanted to go to Toledo. Not only that, your computer's all screwed up. It says I never got on the plane and now my bags are going to Denver."

"What's your name; I'll just look at my terminal."

"Ed Axelrod, goddamn it!"

"Yes, Mr. Axelrod, the record says you never boarded the flight to Toledo."

"But how did I end up in Guam? Look, check my earlier flight from Washington to Cleveland."

"Okay, let me look . . . Yes, apparently you did board the flight that originated in Washington. It's a mystery, alright. Let me call Operations. Please hold."

Twenty minutes later Laurie came back on the line. "Mr. Axelrod, are you still there? Sorry for the delay. Thank you for your patience."

"Where did you think I was? Minneapolis?"

"Mr. Axelrod, I re-checked the computer and someone must have changed your record for the Toledo flight. But Operations can't explain this mishap. They did say that there was unusual sunspot activity during your flight to Toledo, and that communications were disrupted. And there was some damage to some of the seats on the plane."

"So how'd I get to Guam?"

"Operations said it might be a modified cosmic infidibulum. Kurt Vonnegut wrote about them in *The Sirens of Titan*. An infidibulum is a space wave function, or some thingee like that, where people can appear on several planets or moons simultaneously—when those bodies' orbits are in phase with the space wave. But in this case it seems you only appeared in one place at the same time. Operations said that if you wait, you just might go back to Toledo automatically, when the physics change."

"Look, I can't wait. I have to be in Toledo for a morning meeting. And I need my documents."

"Well, okay, Operations said I could give you a complimentary seat on our next flight to Los Angeles from Guam. It leaves in ninety minutes. From LAX, I can connect you to a nonstop to Cleveland and then on to Toledo. How's that sound?"

"What about my appointment?"

"Well, it's tomorrow in Guam. With the time change, you should make it back in the morning."

"Okay."

"Great, you have seat 37C on National flight 12. The flight is full or I'd upgrade you. I did upgrade your flight from LAX to Cleveland. The ticket counter in Guam will give you a complete set of boarding passes. Meanwhile, I'll ask Denver to send your bags back to Toledo. Have a nice flight."

●●●

That afternoon there was another solar eruption. Fourteen passengers were missing when National 12 landed at LAX.

A Sure Thing

Rick Martin's Moonlight Café and Bar, on McNamara Road, was the place to party in Anderson County, Texas. Good drinks, the best barbecue south of Galveston, stunning women, a rocking band, and generous slot machines, made for large and happy crowds. The daily Greyhound, from New Orleans to Corpus Christi, took a dinner break at Rick's; the large gravel parking lot also accommodated eighteen-wheelers. Rick's quarter slot machines, the only one-armed bandits in the county, hummed.

Each machine took in about thirty dollars an hour, and returned twenty-five dollars to the customers—yielding a profit of five dollars. With ten slots, operating six hours nightly, Rick made three hundred dollars a night on his machines.

But Rick had problems. The Christian Women against Gambling (CWAG), led by a local religious fanatic, Sister Bertha Williamson, had demonstrated against gambling often in front of Rick's. CWAG had also petitioned the county supervisors for a hearing, to air its grievances. Rick knew there was a meeting coming up, but he hated politics and couldn't be bothered. He was confident things would stay the same. After all, the Moonlight Café and Bar, just south of the county seat, Quail Vale, had been in Rick's family for three generations.

His grandfather had left it to his dad and Rick had assumed responsibility for the business when his dad retired. Rick was forty-five, thin, six feet tall, and he had some gray in his hair. Despite a mild limp, from being thrown by a horse, he ran three miles daily, worked out with weights, and rode his favorite palomino weekly. There were plenty of women, but Rick's true loves were the slots, and the math that drove them.

Rick had attended the University of Nevada and studied applied math. After graduation, he'd worked as an engineer, at Gally's Slot Machine Manufacturing Company. Rick could fine tune a slot machine to return any percentage; subject only to the laws of statistics and large numbers. Yet few of Rick's customers complained; his slots returned approximately eighty-four percent. The house only took sixteen percent.

The law left Rick's place alone. Slots were legal in Anderson County. He ran a clean shop; prostitution was discouraged; bar fights were squashed; the toilets were clean; the liquor license was legit; and the kitchen always received a stamp of approval from the county inspectors. Further, Rick's Moonlight Café and Bar sat on unincorporated land; the only law enforcement came from Sheriff Kepler. He was a good natured man whose favorite arrests were DUI and speeding—he'd persuaded the county supervisors to set the speed limit on McNamara Road to fifty-three miles per hour. Half the speedometers in the county didn't work and, on busy nights, the sheriff would stash his arrests in Rick's storm cellar, until he'd assembled a large enough group to fill a wagon to ship up to the county jail in Quail Vale.

●●●

One morning in June, Rick jogged up McNamara Road into Quail Vale. When he stopped for a cup of coffee in the Quail Run Coffee Shop, he noticed a shocking headline on the *Anderson County Gazette*. He grabbed a copy and, over coffee, read:

SUPES SLUG SLOTS
(Quail Vale, June 19)

Emotions ran high last night in a meeting of the Anderson County Board of Supervisors. An unlikely coalition of the Christian Women against Gambling (CWAG), headed by local activist Sister Bertha Williamson, and the Association of Choctaw, Chippewa, and Apache Chiefs (CCAC), demanded that the supervisors outlaw gambling in the county. Sister Bertha spoke on the evils of gambling, and the impact it had on the poor and homeless in the county. She said, "These people risk it all on Rick Martin's one-armed bandits. Their children are left helpless, and thrown on the county's welfare system, which can ill afford it."

Chief Running Red Hawk, from Deer Prairie, a large Choctaw reservation near Corpus Christi, represented the CCAC. He said that small-time casinos presented insurmountable political problems to the Indian nations, which wished to negotiate revisions to their treaties with the United States. Such revisions, he claimed, would permit large scale casinos on tribal lands. In response to questions posed by Sister Bertha's followers, he said the poor would not be permitted to enter CCAC Indian casinos. He promised a "Means Test" to protect those less fortunate.

> Supervisor Bob Jenkins asked if anyone wished to speak against the motion to outlaw slot machines. He noted that Rick Martin had been invited to the meeting but that he'd ignored the notice. Several of the supervisors spoke against the motion. Nevertheless, after heated debate, the supervisors voted three to two, with four abstentions, to outlaw slot machines effective August 1st.
>
> At the end of the meeting, there was loud applause from a crowd of CWAG women. The women held hands, and sang 'We Shall Overcome.' Sister Bertha addressed her followers saying, "Next, we go after the firewater."

Oh my God, Rick thought, this could cost him a hundred grand a year. *And they're going after the booze next?* The threats elicited panic. He gulped down his coffee and ran over to the county jail. Sheriff Kepler was hanging a wanted poster on the bulletin board when Rick barged in.

"Sheriff, what can I do about this new law against slots?"

"Rick, I wondered why you weren't at the meeting. CWAG had the audience wired, but most people in the county like you; I'm sure the supervisors would have rejected the law; if you'd argued against it."

"Well, I'm gonna fight it anyway. My dad's lawyer is up in Galveston, and I'm going there today."

Sheriff Kepler frowned and shook his head. "Those machines will be illegal in August. You better get rid of them. I'm sworn to uphold the law; I don't want to have to arrest you."

Rick felt his bile rising. "You do what you got to do. You better find a new place to stow your drunks. As of now, my storm cellar is off-limits."

"Sorry you feel that way, Rick."

● ● ●

Rick's visit to the lawyer proved fruitless. "We can appeal it," said the lawyer, "but we'll lose. I recommend you save the legal fees and forfeit the machines. Meanwhile, you should pay more attention to those notices of hearings in the future; you don't want the county going dry on you."

● ● ●

July came and went, and Rick dithered. Each slot generated thirty; sometimes fifty dollars a night. Business was so good he considered installing more machines. Salesmen from Gally's encouraged him to fight the new ordinance.

Unable to make a decision, Rick kept his machines. It was difficult to abandon an income stream of five hundred dollars a night. But Rick knew it wouldn't last forever.

On August 8th, Sheriff Kepler arrived in a convoy of two police cruisers and a large U-Haul truck. He served a warrant, ordered his deputies to confiscate the machines, and told Rick to present himself in the courthouse the next morning—to be booked on a charge of illegal gambling. The band departed and half an hour later, the Moonlight Café and Bar was deserted.

The next day Rick was booked, fingerprinted, and released on his own recognizance. He was sitting at one of his tables, pondering his future, when Jesse James Johnson, a horse trainer and old cowboy, sat down with a beer.

"What'ya gonna do, Rick?"

"Beats the shit out of me, Jesse. I need to replace a hundred thousand a year or I'm out of business."

"Well, I don't have any business ideas, but I got a hot tip. *Incitatus*, in the third, at Belmont, on the 12th of August, is a sure thing."

"A sure thing? How is that possible?" Rick was looking at an empty wall where his slot machines once stood; now they, he thought ruefully—*they* were a sure thing.

Jesse grinned. "There ain't no one that knows horseflesh better than me; and I'm telling you, it's a sure thing. And, when there's no risk, it ain't gambling!"

At that moment something clicked in Rick's brain and he had an epiphany—if it was a sure thing, if there was no risk, it wasn't gambling!! He grabbed the phone and called the chief engineer at Gally's.

"Let me ask you a question. Is it possible—?"

● ● ●

Six weeks later, Rick's Moonlight Café and Bar was jumping. Ten new slot machines were aligned along the wall. The band was playing, people were dancing, beer was flowing, and everyone was having a good time. Quarters were dropping into the slots, which still paid out eighty-four percent; just under slightly different conditions than usual.

At 10 pm the sheriff pulled up in his cruiser. He was alone this time, and he asked Rick to step outside.

The two men leaned against the side of the cruiser. There were gray dust clouds floating in the air, illuminated by the mercury vapor lights, and stirred up by the sheriff, who kicked repeatedly, at the gravel, with the tips of his boots.

"Rick, what's this bullshit? These slots are illegal."

"Sheriff," Rick said with confidence, "these machines may look like traditional slots, but they're not illegal. They're nothing but mechanical games, like pinball machines. There's no risk and you know exactly what will happen, before you put in a quarter."

The sheriff acted bewildered. "What do you mean?"

"C'mon, I'll show you."

They went back inside and walked up to one of the new machines. It looked like a standard slot machine; it had three wheels and a big arm.

"Look at this machine," said Rick. "The wheels at the pay-line show cherry-apple-watermelon, right?

"Er, yes."

"Well, according to the pay-table on the front, that means the machine will pay you two quarters, if you put in one quarter. It's determined in advance. Try it."

The sheriff put a quarter in the slot, pulled the arm, and received two quarters in return. This time the wheels at the pay-line displayed bar-bar-lemon.

"The pay-table," said Rick "tells you that if you put a quarter in, you get back nothing. That's also completely determined, in advance. There's no uncertainty, so it can't be gambling. Try it."

The sheriff dutifully put in one of the two quarters and the machine gobbled it up and yielded nothing. The wheels moved into new positions.

"Well, what about the next roll?" asked the sheriff.

"What about it? Don't they call that speculation in the law? No one says you got to speculate."

"But Rick, they're gambling; they're just betting they'll get a winner on the next roll."

"So let's see, the wheels say there's no payout, but somebody puts money in the machine anyway. You say that's illegal? Since when is it illegal to be stupid?"

"But what about the poor people? What if they're down to their last quarter?"

Rick smiled. "Now that would be really dumb, wouldn't it? To put your last quarter in the machine; when you know, without doubt, that it's a loser?" Rick figured that's what happened with this machine; some fool had put in his last quarter.

"I can't deal with this logic," said Kepler. "I got to report this to the supervisors. This is way above my pay grade."

"You do that, Sheriff. Have a nice evening."

● ● ●

After the sheriff reported, the county supervisors consulted with District Attorney Alex Lohse. He said that Rick's argument was interesting but the local county court would reject it. "The problem," noted Lohse, "will come if, and when, Rick appeals it to a higher court, where there might be thinking creatures."

The supervisors decided to ask Judge Barney Green to issue a warrant to confiscate the new machines. Sheriff Kepler was ordered to grab them. At a hearing, to determine the status of the new slots, Judge Green ruled the machines were gaming devices. Rick, after consulting with a legal scholar at the University of Texas, decided to bring a case in Federal Court, on constitutional grounds.

●●●

Several months later, a troupe of lawyers from the American Civil Liberties Union marched into the U.S. District Court for Southern Texas, in Galveston. The ACLU represented Rick; the county was represented by Alex Lohse. The case was called by Judge William Kennedy.

"I understand this case is being argued on constitutional grounds. Is that correct?"

"Yes, Your Honor," said the lead ACLU lawyer. "We believe that the definition of gambling is so explicit, and the law so vague regarding enforcement, as to render it unconstitutional in this case."

"Well, what is the definition of gambling?" asked the judge.

"If I may, Your Honor, we've assembled definitions of gambling from several sources. Gambling is: the act of playing for stakes in the hopes of winning, to bet on an act or undertaking of uncertain outcome, to play a game of chance for stakes, any matter or thing involving risk or uncertainty, and a person must have something at risk to be considered gambling."

"Your Honor," he continued, "this is only the tip of the iceberg. Every definition requires unpredictability, risk, chance, and uncertainty."

"All right, thank you. And why does that not apply in this case?"

"Your Honor, our client, Rick Martin, did not operate games of chance. In every instance, in every play, the player knew precisely, in advance, what would happen. May we demonstrate?"

With the judge's permission, one of Rick's new slot machines was wheeled into the courtroom. The ACLU attorney pulled the arm ten times. The machine swallowed ten quarters, and spat out a total of seven quarters.

Rick's attorney said, "Your Honor, I hope you noted that at every step we knew precisely what would happen, in advance. It might be dumb to insert those quarters, but it is not gambling, by any definition."

"Thank you. Mr. Lohse, what say the county?"

"Judge, the county submits that the devices owned by Mr. Martin are gambling machines; that the players assume risk on the next roll of the machine."

The ACLU lawyer leapt up. "I object. What is this 'next roll' stuff? That's speculation, pure and simple. At no time, in the act of using the machine is there uncertainty. How do we know the player thinks that he wants to know what the next roll will be? What if the player just likes to watch wheels spin and lights flash, like people who watch a pinball machine? How can we get inside the head of the player? The only thing that is certain is the predetermined result on our client's machine."

Judge Kennedy pondered the argument. "Objection noted. I will take the case under advisement. Briefs in two weeks," he ordered. "Replies, if any, in two more."

● ● ●

Six months later, Judge Kennedy ruled that Rick's new slots were not gaming devices. Rick's patent application, filed after his epiphany, was approved. Most casinos in the country based their slot machines on Rick's patent. The Indian tribes were happy; by substituting Rick's non-gambling machines for their existing slots, they could ignore the restrictions placed on them by the State Gaming Commissions. By paying Rick royalties, they dramatically increased the number of machines in their casinos. Rick was a wealthy man.

Coolidge Said

Sloan answered the phone.

"Sloan, is that you? The feds are on to us. Get rid of all the data!"

"All of it, the files and the e-mails?"

"Yes. If they get that shit we're all going to jail—for life! Enron was a joke compared to what they'll do to us."

Sloan hung up, scared, and called the *Geek Squad*.

Later, an orange and black Volkswagen from the *Geek Squad* pulled into Sloan's driveway. Leslie 'Lizzie' McCain, senior systems analyst, retrieved her flash memory stick off the rear seat of her car and walked up to Sloan's door.

Sloan answered before the knock.

"Mr. Sloan? Hi! My name is Lizzie. I'm from the *Geek Squad*. I believe you called us; you need some help with your computer?"

"Lizzie, it's nice to meet you. Come in, come in, please. I got to erase some files and e-mail messages—you might say that I need to get rid of some incriminating files, ha-ha!"

Sloan checked the street for strange cars as he closed the door and chained it.

"Don't concern yourself, Mr. Sloan," said Lizzie with a smile. "We don't care what's in the files. Can you show me to the computer?"

"Yes, it's a Dell something. I have a connection to the Internet—whatever that is. I don't really know how it all works, but I can write Word files and do e-mail."

"Well that sounds like a useful system, Mr. Sloan. I take it you run Windows on it?"

"Yeah, I think so. Let me show you the stuff that I need to get rid of."

Lizzie frowned. "Mr. Sloan, although we can erase that stuff—as you call it, you do understand, don't you, that just deleting the files won't make them go totally away?"

"What? Jesus! I thought all I had to do was delete them and the computer would work its magic. I only called you guys because someone on that TV show, *CSI*, mentioned hard drives; in one of the episodes."

"Let's see if I can explain. When you delete a file, it releases the memory, does away with pointers to it, and makes it difficult to retrieve. That means the programs, or if you prefer, the things that use the file, like your printer, can no longer find it. But it doesn't literally erase the information."

"What's a pointer?" Sloan felt blood pounding in his ears and wiped his forehead with a handkerchief.

"That's not important," she said. "The thing is the characters in the computer's memory still retain the original information, and they'll continue to retain that information, until they're overwritten."

"I thought you said it releases the memory. Shit. Doesn't it go away forever?"

"Well, then eventually all your computer memory would disappear. That's not how it works."

"So what do I have to do to get rid of the information?" Sloan thought he was on the verge of a spontaneous nosebleed.

"Well, we find a way to overwrite it with ones and zeros."

"Can you do that?" he asked nervously.

"No problem. We have software tools for that."

"And this software tool you're going to use; is it different than hardware?"

"Yes, I have some here in my flash memory."

"Well, that looks like hardware to me. It's hard, isn't it?"

"Mr. Sloan, perhaps you can give me some time and I'll delete those Word files for good for you."

●●●

"Okay, Mr. Sloan. Those files have been deleted and overwritten."

"Thanks," said a somewhat relieved Sloan. "Now, can we move on to my e-mail messages? They're much more dangerous . . . er . . . I mean important. I have about two hundred of them that I need to destroy; half sent and half received."

"Well, it's the same problem, only worse. We can destroy the messages on your computer. But you understand, don't you, that there are still copies of the messages out there in the ether?"

"Huh? What's ether? What do you mean? How can there be copies. Someone sends me a message; I receive it—and that's it, isn't it?" Sloan's nose began to bleed and he dabbed at it with his handkerchief.

"No, I'm afraid not," said Lizzie. "Do you know how a packet-switched network works?"

"What's a packet?"

"Mr. Sloan, this visit is going to get expensive. Perhaps I can explain using layman terms. When someone sends you an e-mail message, it gets broken up into little pieces—we call them packets—and those packets get sent over the Internet to your service provider—to your ISP."

"So, what's the problem?" Sloan's handkerchief had a large red splotch.

"Well, as the packets move through the Internet, parts of them are stored and forwarded a number of times on different servers. It depends on your distance from the sender and lots of other things."

"Like what?"

"Well, to give an absurd example, it could depend on sun spots."

"Who gives a shit about sun spots?" Sloan's nose was bleeding and this crazy broad was talking about sun spots?

"Well, anyway, eventually your ISP gets the message and sends it to your computer. In this whole process there are many copies made of the message. Not to mention that the original e-mail message might still be on the sender's machine—"

"Lizzie, I'm confused. You're telling me those copies are still out there? But there must be billions. How can they keep all of them? Can't we just delete them on my machine and send a message to delete them on all those, what did you call them, servers?"

"No, we can't do that. We can only erase them on your machine."

"What if I send a new email message with just ones and zeros? Can't that overwrite those messages out there?" Sloan's shirt was drenched in sweat; he needed a drink.

"That's a novel thought, Mr. Sloan but it won't work. You see that new message would get stored in a new place, well, actually, in many new places, with new pointers."

"Goddamn pointers, whatever they are. So let's see if I understand you. I can erase my computer, overwrite the memory, beat the crap out of the box with a sledgehammer, and the feds can still read my e-mails?"

"There's no need to be crude, Mr. Sloan. But, alas, that's true. The only way to protect the words is to not create them in the first place."

"You don't understand, oh Christ, never mind—"

● ● ●

Flashing red lights bounced off the Dell's screen. The room was awash with men in uniforms.

"That's right, officer," said Lizzie. "Mr. Sloan pulled out a gun and shot himself. It was horrible. He bled all over his computer printer and I called you immediately."

The policeman nodded. "What happened to cause this tragedy?"

"He had a problem understanding the concept of erasing computer memory."

"I don't understand it either. But what was his problem?"

"He said that he had some information he wanted to permanently delete. I was trying to explain how it worked, and I paraphrased President Coolidge. Perhaps if Mr. Sloan had been a student of history this wouldn't have happened."

"What did President Coolidge say?"

"If you don't say it, they can't ask you to repeat it."

"Well, I guess we better bring in the feds. Can you give me a copy of what's on the machine?"

"Well, the e-mail files are right there and we can print them. You'll have to put new paper in the printer, of course. Unfortunately I overwrote the Word files. But, wait . . . Damn, I forgot the backup files so, sure, we just have to restore the information on the hard drive."

The Piano Police

Davey Grant was six years old, small for his age, and frightened of everything: his shadow, dogs, bullies, and smelly things like cooked cauliflower. And, if being small and terrified weren't enough, he was afraid of his new piano teacher. Baron Szily was a Hungarian—a descendant of a minor branch of a noble family in the days of the Habsburgs—with an eye patch and a wooden foot.

Szily spoke with a strange accent, never smiled, and wore a cape just like that bad guy, Dracula who had scared Davey in *Abbot and Costello Meet Frankenstein*; the scariest DVD that Davey had ever seen. Szily clumped around like the monster, Frankenstein, too.

Davey had been taking piano lessons at the Lafayette Music School since he was four and had progressed rapidly. Despite his skill, he had a problem counting out loud as he played his music. His reticence to count had become a larger and larger problem as the music increased in complexity. Davey's previous teacher had been relaxed and encouraging, but this new teacher was more demanding and difficult.

Davey was struggling in his piano lesson one day when the baron barked, "David, you must count! One and two and three and one and—"

Davey slammed his hands on the keyboard, striking discordant notes that reverberated throughout the room. He looked at his teacher with fear, anger, and frustration. "I hate to count. Hate it. It's so hard, it sounds stupid, and all my friends laugh at me."

Szily, who had studied under someone who had studied under the master Carl Czerny, shook his head. These Americans! he thought. Spoiled rotten by their wealth and privilege. How could they ever understand the demands that music, fine music, placed on them? He rolled his one eye, snorted in disgust, and tried once more. "Counting, David, is absolutely necessary to play the music properly. Someday you might count in your head but for now, you must say it out loud. If you don't count, the Piano Police will get angry. Do you see my foot? That's what happens when the Piano Police get angry."

The baron's right foot was a large hunk of carved red wood which he lifted and slammed down with a loud *thunk* on every other step. Davey pictured himself trying to run to first base with a wooden foot and all the kids laughing at him. He gulped, with tears in his eyes. "I'll try. Please don't call the Piano Police." He wondered if he could reach the pedals if he had a wooden foot.

"At your recital this weekend I will expect to hear you counting every beat of the music. Beethoven's *Für Elise* is a beautiful piece when it is properly timed. Now be sure to practice for another hour while you count. I will see you Saturday." The baron stood up, draped his cape over his shoulders, and stormed out of the room with a series of thunks.

Davey gritted his teeth and turned back to his music. Those Piano Police meant he had to count. He liked his right foot. Crestfallen, he practiced his A-minor scale and counted every beat while he ran his fingers up and down the notes. Then he doubled the speed and counted twice as fast as he went up and down two full octaves. Then he tripled the speed and the octaves and the numbers poured out of his mouth. It sounded awful.

●●●

"So how's he doing?" asked Mr. Grant, Davey's father. He'd stopped Baron Szily as he limped and banged his way down the hallway of the Lafayette Music School. Mr. Grant didn't like Szily but he knew the baron was a good pianist.

"He's doing just fine but he must have more discipline."

"But Baron, he's only six years old. He can't even reach the pedals."

"Music demands perfection!"

Despite his distaste for the man's personality, Grant knew that Szily had been shot and wounded as he escaped Hungary, in the 1956 Revolution. Grant wondered if that experience had turned Szily into a demanding teacher or whether the man always had been plagued by an obsession with perfection—which Grant knew was groomed and reinforced in classical musicians. After all, the man was a disciple of the Czerny school.

"I know he's afraid of you, Baron. I'm not sure that's the way to motivate the boy."

The baron stopped and turned to face Grant. He poked his finger in Grant's chest. "Bah! The boy has nothing to fear. I merely stressed the need to count the notes. But he is just, I suspect, another unsophisticated American. You should dampen your expectations."

Mr. Grant nodded. "Baron, I want the best for Davey. And you should relax sometimes."

●●●

That Saturday afternoon the Lafayette Music School's students and parents assembled for the recital. Davey waited for his turn. The big clock on the auditorium wall said 2:30 and Davey knew he had another half hour. His eyes searched the audience but they kept returning to the baron's red cape. Davey's stomach churned as he watched the sweep hand count off the seconds. He wished he was in bed.

●●●

Bill Collins and Crazy Joe Franklin, good ole boys in the local Knights of the Klan, were driving down a dirt road on the outskirts of Lafayette. Bill's .22 rifle obscured the view in the rear window, but Joe could see Thor, Bill's German shepherd, standing in the bed of the truck. The dog was drooling with his tongue hanging out. The truck raised large clouds of yellow dust that coated Thor and left tire tracks that looked like a huge python had slithered down the road.

Sweat stains marched across Joe's T-shirt.

"Who cares if you owe Dutch that money?" asked Bill, who was half snookered on moonshine and driving erratically. "He's a pussy and it's only a grand—so what's the big deal?" Bill's eyes squinted as he looked at the clock on the dashboard of his '79 Chevy pick-up. The numbers seemed to quiver. It was 2:35. In the fifteen minutes that Crazy Joe had been in the truck, they'd consumed two-thirds of the White Lightning in Bill's Mason jar. Moonshine made Joe nuttier than usual and Bill already regretted picking him up.

"He may be a pushover," said Joe, "but he's got tough friends. Jose, that spic buddy of his, can bench press three hundred pounds and he'll be in my face if I don't pay off Dutch."

"So what you gonna do?" asked Bill nervously.

Joe swallowed more moonshine and passed the bottle to Bill. "I don't know. Let's see if we can solve the problem in that 7-11 in Lafayette."

"Are you sure? They got tough cops in Lafayette and the sheriff is one mean SOB, too."

Joe smiled and reached into the glove compartment for Bill's Colt .380 semi-automatic. It was a small handgun holding five rounds in the magazine and one in the pipe. "Don't worry. We'll be in and out in no time at all."

●●●

Twenty minutes later a beautician in a shop next to a 7-11 heard a shot. She saw two men run past her window and jump into an old Chevy pick-up. There was a snarling German shepherd in the bed of the truck and it had a bumper sticker that read: "Help Stamp out Bumper Stickers." She called the sheriff.

Bill and Joe were speeding away with $183. Bill shook as the 7-11 vanished in his rear view mirror. "Damn it Joe, did you have to shoot the clerk? That's all the money he had in the cash drawer."

"I didn't like his attitude. Look, we got to get more money. Head for the currency exchange in Fort Wayne."

"Why don't we just get drunk, instead? We're in deep shit now. This is serious stuff."

"Look Bill, I'm sorry. It's that goddamn Dutch. I got to get more money. What else could I do?" Joe began waving the .380 in the air.

"Jesus, be careful. It's loaded." Bill wondered if he should just ditch Joe. Let the stupid bastard keep the truck while he headed for the hills.

Just then the men heard a siren whoop. Bill looked in his mirror and saw a sheriff's deputy cruiser racing towards them. In the distance he could see another cruiser with flashing lights. He floored the accelerator. Thor howled and the two men looked at each other.

"Goddamn it Joe. What are we gonna do?"

"Let's ditch the truck and hide out in that school over there."

●●●

The audience applauded as Davey Grant walked onto the stage with his sheet music. There were suppressed giggles in the crowd as he sat on the piano bench with dangling feet. A proud Mr. Grant sat in the front row while Baron Szily, with his usual frown, had a seat in the last row, on the aisle.

Davey opened his sheet music and prepared to play. The crowd hushed and he began, hoping that the music would drown out the sound of his counting. He played well but, as he came to the end of the second page, he slowed to turn the page. He reached for the sheet music and fumbled it. This caused him to stop counting so that no one would hear him. Baron Szily jumped out of his seat and stormed down the aisle shouting: "Count, I told you to count." Davey heard thunk! Thunk! Thunk! He froze in fear, picturing Frankenstein.

Two men with a gun burst into the auditorium followed by three armed deputies. Davey saw the police and became hysterical. His right leg jerked as he hyperventilated and fell off the piano bench. Lying on the floor, Davey's eyes filled with the vision of three policemen coming to take off his right foot. Bedlam erupted as the crowd panicked. People stormed for the exits, blocking the deputies. Davey heard shouts and he passed out.

The baron turned and was confronted by a man with a gun.

"Get out my way, you stupid cripple," snarled the gunman, "or I'll shoot you."

Baron Szily could see the police fighting their way through the seething crowd. He stiffened. "That's my student up there. There is no way I will let you pass. I saw enough scum like you in Communist Hungary. Get—"

The gunman shot the baron in the stomach. He fired again and the shot went wild, striking Davey in the right foot. The baron, as he fell, wrapped his arms around the gunman's legs and dragged him to the floor. Mr. Grant sprang up and raced for the stage. By the time he got to Davey, who was still unconscious, the gunman's accomplice had surrendered to the deputies. Two ambulances arrived in fifteen minutes.

● ● ●

They released Davey from the hospital three days later. His right foot was in a white cast that extended to his knee. Davey was pale and dopey and stared repeatedly at his leg.

As his father wheeled him to the front of the hospital, he asked, "Dad, do I still have my foot?"

"Of course, Davey."

"Are you sure?"

"Why would you even think that?"

Davey nodded and decided to believe his father. Still, those Piano Police had come . . .

What happened to my teacher?"

"The baron? He'll be in the hospital for some time. You know, he may have saved your life. He was shot but he still helped the police catch the man with the gun."

"Dad, I don't want to play the piano anymore."

"But Davey, I can get you a different teacher."

"It's not the teacher. I don't like to count. The baron told me the Piano Police would come for me, if I didn't count, and they did."

Davey's father nodded. He grabbed Davey's hand to reassure him. "It's okay, Davey," he said, both loathing and loving the man that had stopped the gunman. "The Piano Police will never come again."

Gravity

Joe, an inveterate inventor, was excited. His last experiment worked. The garage floor was littered with empty bottles, spilled liquids, overturned buckets, and empty soup cans. But, despite the staggering mess, Joe burst with enthusiasm when someone knocked on the garage door.

Joe opened the door. "Don, you came!"

"What else? Your call sounded urgent."

"It was—"

Don wrinkled his nose. "What's that smell?"

"Oh, nothing. I had a goat in here for a day."

"A goat?"

"Forget it. I tell you the damn thing works. I turned it on and I could feel it pulling me."

"Sure, sure, that little box has gravity! What have you been snorting?"

"Look, put that ball over there near the box and I'll turn it on again."

Don couldn't believe he was going along with the farce but he walked dutifully over to the table in the garage, moved a small red handball a few inches away from Joe's Rube Goldberg box, and waited expectantly.

"Now watch this," said Joe, with a wide grin on his face.

Joe plugged an extension cord into the wall. Don heard a motor spin up and the handball rocketed over and hung against the side of the box. Don also felt a strong tug, in the direction of the box. Joe pulled the plug out; the ball bounced on the table and fell to the floor, dribbling away. The tug on Don dissipated.

"Well, I'll be damned, How does it work?"

"It's based on some Einstein stuff. He said that light bends in a gravitational field. I figured maybe that it would work backwards; you know; bend light and create gravity. The more light you bend; the more gravity you get—that's the theory."

"But how do you bend it? You can't use a mirror, can you? Don't that absorb all that gravity stuff?"

"Right," said Joe. "I tried a mirror, but apparently you need to use something mechanical to bend the light. I tried all kinds of different ways to bend it; magnets, smoke, prisms, everything. Finally, I tried spinning a Folger's coffee can and bouncing light off of different fluids. When I combined the spinning can with a red filtered spotlight, it worked. It even works with a red flashlight but I thought that plugging it into the wall would be, you know, more dramatic."

"What kind of fluid did you use?" asked Don. He saw empty bottles stashed on the shelves, on the counters, under the tables, and scattered around the floor. There was a pile of what looked like dog poop in the corner, with flies buzzing around.

"Boy, talk about problems. I started with water, went through apple juice, V8, Goat's milk, Clorox, Campbell's Chicken Noodle soup, olive oil, and half a dozen different Chardonnays. It finally worked when I used dog piss."

"You're using dog piss?" Don was incredulous.

"Not only that; it has to come from a Chihuahua."

"This is fantastic. Have you tried bouncing it twice?"

"No, actually I'm afraid to. I'm concerned it might double, or quadruple the force."

"Well, if it does that you'll get the Nobel Prize in physics. Let's try. Do you have another coffee can?"

The men took another Folger's coffee can and mounted it on a second motor drive inside Joe's box. They pointed the second can at the first can.

"How much dog piss does it take?" asked Don.

"I used a half a cup."

"Let's use a pint this time. Don was excited as he poured a pint of Chihuahua dog piss into the can. He wondered where all the dog piss came from.

"Hey, it's a good thing you had more dog piss."

"Yeah," said Joe. "It cost a bundle. Are you ready? Should I plug the box in again?"

"You know; they didn't know what would happen at Yucca Flats either, when they tested the A-bomb. Maybe we'll get an earthquake or something. We should take good notes."

"That's a good idea, Don. Start writing. I'll plug the sucker in."

Joe's gravity pump began to spin up; the red beam bounced back and forth between the two coffee cans at the speed of light; and the force was magnified exponentially, on every other bounce, by the extra dog piss.

FLASH!!!!

Two years later, astronomers on a small planet circling Draconnis 3, a star in the Crab Nebula galaxy, were startled by a new black hole. The mysterious hole sat on the edge of the Andromeda galaxy, called the Milky Way on an extinct, blue-green planet. The black hole's gravitational field was slowly sucking seven other planets, their moons, and the third class star, about which they rotated, into the hole.

Four Stars

★ ★ ★ ★

Lieutenant General Samuel "Beer" Adams, U.S. Army, director of the National Security Agency, and third in his class at West Point, enjoyed a snooze after a big lunch in his office, on the ninth floor of the headquarters building. The sun shone through the windows and the TV monitors were off. Except for a few command and control displays, all was serene.

Suddenly, the door burst open and a host of people barged in. The new Speaker of the House, Nancy Girabaldi, left-wing darling of San Francisco values, led the charge, followed by her entourage consisting of her political advisor, scribe, photographer, hairdresser, cosmetician, plus two secret service men, detailed to her by the White House.

What the hell?

"General Adams? Please excuse this unannounced interruption but it's impossible to get your telephone number—you know all that silly top secret stuff."

"Madame, this is a classified area. Where are your badges? You need a clearance to be in here." The general swept all the papers on his desk into a drawer.

"Oh, don't be ridiculous, General. We didn't sign in. I make the appointments to the Intelligence committees; I can give myself all the clearances I want. And badges are so déclassé—as if they really matter."

"They matter to me."

"All right, big deal!" She turned to her entourage. "You can all leave."

"What's this about Madame Speaker?"

General Adams reached for his phone, intending to call the MPs, but Girabaldi smiled sweetly. "General, how would you like a fourth star? Please put the phone down."

Adams cradled the phone. "You barged into NSA headquarters, dragged half of Washington with you, broke about a half-dozen national security laws, to offer me another star? Please, Madame Speaker, this is an Intelligence agency."

"That's what I want to discuss with you." She looked around the room. "These are nice digs, General. You spooks sure have a good thing going.

What did that private toilet over there cost—a hundred and fifty thousand dollars?"

"I don't know, Madame Speaker."

"Uh-huh. Well, I have a proposition for you, General. I'd like you to chair my special bi-partisan Intelligence Reorganization Committee."

"I see. Just what are the goals of this lofty committee?"

"I want to reorganize the Intelligence community. Let's say that I believe there is enormous waste. The American people need that money for more pressing things."

"Madame Speaker, it sounds to me like you want to do away with Intelligence! And you're offering me a fourth star to sell it down the river?"

"General, your colleagues don't seem to have a problem. I've already secured the participation of Major General Smith of the Army Intelligence Command, Rear Admiral Jones of the Naval Intelligence Service, and Major General Hook of the Defense Intelligence Agency. They all said they'd be pleased to serve on your committee—I took the liberty of telling them you were on-board."

Adams gagged. *This must be how Admiral Kimmel felt when the Japs bombed Pearl Harbor. Those guys must think I'm nuts.* "Madame Speaker, just what does reorganization mean, precisely?"

"I'm glad you asked. I want to merge all the military Intelligence agencies, NSA and the CIA. I figure we can save about seventy, maybe eighty billion dollars a year doing that. As Senator Dirksen once said, 'a billion here and a' ... well you know ... 'after a while it adds up to real money.' If we also retire a few naval carrier groups, we can get to one hundred billion dollars. Just think of all the good things we could do with a tenth of a trillion dollars. We could increase the minimum wage!"

The General felt his temperature rise. *She may want a tenth of something but I could use a fifth of something else, right now.* He sensed his blood pressure rising. "What does the CIA think about this?"

"I haven't talked to them yet. Actually, I thought that with your fourth star you could take over the new integrated agency."

"Madame Speaker, cuts in spending like that will devastate the Intelligence community, not to mention the Navy. You do know, don't you, that President Clinton cut the spending drastically on Intelligence in the Nineties, and the result was 9/11?"

"Oh, please, you military types—you always mention 9/11. Listen, General, the American people don't give a shit about 9/11. They want jobs! Better social security. Medicare. And education; they need more money for education!"

The general tried to control his temper which, at the moment, was moving toward a volcanic eruption. "Listen here, Madame Speaker. Every time you politicians throw more money at education, student performance goes in the crapper. What you need to do is reduce spending and performance will go up!"

"I didn't come here to argue with you. We have an aggressive legislative agenda and we're going to save this country. Why should Americans die for those miserable countries in far-away places?"

"Madame Speaker, have you ever read history? Do you know that the British and the French, in 1938, said those very same words about Czechoslovakia? That one only cost about eighty million lives."

"General, we're making history. Do you want the job or not? I don't have all day. I have to be in Langley in two hours and I need to tell those idiots something."

General Adams pondered the lunatic in front of him for a few moments. "Would you like a cup of coffee, Madame Speaker? I need to think about this."

"Actually I'd prefer tea, if you don't mind. Mango Ceylon decaffeinated tea."

"Yes, of course." The general picked up his phone and ordered the tea and a cup of coffee. There was an awkward moment while they waited, and Adams glared out the window.

A few moments later an aide delivered the beverages.

"So Madame Speaker, if I agree, what happens next?"

"We bring in the photographer and take a picture shaking hands. Then I go to Langley, dump on them, have my hair done, and call a press conference. The American people will be thrilled with these savings! Just think of all those hot lunches, new educational programs, and free universal health care!"

"That would be nice, Madame Speaker. I'm certain that your party will garner many more votes in the next election. Perhaps you could include funds for retraining the Intelligence workers that will lose their jobs, too."

"General, of course! Worker retraining is a keystone of any Democratic agenda. I can't tell you how excited I am at this plan. And this tea is wonderful. Let's bring in the photographer."

Adams sighed, gritted his teeth, pulled his 1907 Colt .45 service piece out of his desk drawer, and fired two rounds into Speaker Girabaldi's head. When the secret service detail stormed into his office, he surrendered the weapon. In response to the bewildered looks, he said, "It felt like I was in a Stephen King story. I just saved America."

Tiger!

The divers were asleep—scattered around the rear of the Boeing 737 cabin. The Air Pacific flight to Fiji had left Honolulu at midnight. Sprawled in an aisle seat, Don Leatherman snored with his mouth open. Everyone around him had stuffed plugs in their ears and drunk themselves to sleep.

Don was stocky with the body of a weightlifter. He had enormous arms from lifting thousands of tanks of compressed air in his dive shop on Maui. Don's Dive Shop was the preferred diving establishment for the locals in Kihei, as well as knowledgeable divers from the mainland.

The shop was known for its friendly environment, impeccable attention to detail, and excellent diving instructors. Attesting to that popularity were nineteen people on board who'd subscribed to Don's annual trip to Beqa Island. A new Open Water certified diver, Bill Casey, twenty-nine, rolled over and poked Don in the ribs with an elbow. Don awoke with a grunt.

"Yo, Bill, what's up?"

"Sorry. Accident."

"No problem. Tell me Bill, are you going to the Shark Feed?"

"Gee, I don't know. That's scary stuff."

"Aw, come on," said Don, as he raised his seat to an upright position. "I've been doing this for years. The feeds are tame as hell; the sharks are well fed, and there's a bunch of professional divers that act as handlers—in case one of the fish gets nosey."

"It's optional, ain't it? And it costs an extra $100, doesn't it?"

"Yeah, but it's worth it! There will be a herd of Bull Sharks; they're six-to-ten feet long if they're an inch."

Bill flinched. "Jesus! And they're tame?"

"Well, *tame* might be a stretch." Don was smiling.

"Well, how does it work? Do we just jump in the water and watch them eat? What do they eat?"

Don looked at Bill. This was Bill's first trip with Don's Dive Shop. It required only five dives to get to Bill's level of certification and most such divers weren't very competent. They had trouble controlling their buoyancy, they had few specialties such as Navigation or Deep, and they also consumed vast quantities of air. *Maybe we shouldn't take him to the Shark Feed.*

"It's really pretty safe, Bill. They do this once a week. They assemble several boats of divers from the different resorts in Beqa Lagoon and everyone dives together. They do the feed at fifty feet."

"Fifty? That seems deep to me. I only feel safe at thirty-five feet, where I know I can make it to the surface, if I run out of air. You know, just exhaling."

"No one is going to run out of air. There are twenty of us which means there are forty air supply regulators plus the Fiji dive masters and the other boats' divers. The boats drop extra tanks on ropes fifteen feet down with extra regulators. You can hang off of them, if necessary, and perform a safety stop on their air. And it's not like we're going real deep. You just need five minutes and even that's overkill. But, in the worst case, you could stay down a long time."

"So, what happens next?"

"The Fijians have constructed a small wall out of rocks and coral on the bottom and we all collect along one side of the wall. With all of the divers putting up bubbles, we create a seemingly impenetrable wall—no shark is going to come through it. Then some Fiji dive masters stand in front of the wall, and some station themselves behind the divers. These are the handlers, with long poles or spears to discourage any accidental interest. Another guy feeds the sharks. These are Bull Sharks, pretty non-threatening, too." *He doesn't need to know that Bull Sharks are an aggressive and mean species and that they've been known to cruise up the Ganges River feeding on Hindi corpses.*

"Some guy feeds the sharks? How?"

"He digs fish parts out of a portable dumpster, like a yard recycling bin—they call it a chum bucket—and throws the food into the sharks' mouths as they swim by."

"Do these guys have all of their hands? That sounds really stupid."

"Well," said Don, "I agree you got to be careful but diving is supposed to be exciting and it's the professionals who take the risk. Bring your camera and you'll be so busy taking pictures it'll be over in no time."

"And what keeps the sharks from fighting over the food? They line up?"

"That's right. It's like a circus act. The sharks swim in a circle nose to tail, like a daisy chain—similar to elephants walking. They take turns too. They peel out of the circle and make a pass at the food—then they get back in the circle."

"Uh-huh. Six-to-ten foot sharks? Over my dead body." Bill looked at Don like he was out of his mind, pulled the blanket over his head, and rolled over.

"Don't be a wuss, Bill; girls will be there." Don smiled, reclined his seat, closed his eyes, and was snoring again in two minutes.

• • •

Twelve hours later the group was ensconced in the Lawaki Beach House on Beqa Island. The island was situated in a large lagoon about five miles south of Navua, the capital of the main Fiji island of Viti Levu. A reef encircled the island and a barrier reef surrounded the lagoon. Coral was everywhere, radiating vibrant colors and the reefs teemed with tropical fish and other creatures. Diving conditions were good with very warm waters and excellent visibility.

Upon arrival the divers had checked out their gear, enjoyed a welcoming lunch, and were assigned to their own private bungalows, or shared condominiums, along the lagoon. Bill Casey had requested a private room. He'd received a small bungalow with a private plunge pool, right at the beach. He was relaxing in a hammock tied to two palm trees when two women, from the condominiums next door, came by with a bottle of vodka and three glasses. The women had been sitting in the rear of the flight to Fiji and Bill had kidded around with them on the boat ride to Beqa Island.

"Got any ice?" asked Celia, a fine looking woman, thirty-five, with over three hundred dives in her logbook. Her girlfriend, Jennifer was a little younger but Bill thought Jennifer was the prettier of the two. Jennifer was a certified Master Scuba diver with a Rescue Diver specialty.

"Sure," answered Bill. "I already got an ice bucket from the lodge."

In the company of two attractive women, Bill began to relax. The trip was going to last ten days and some female company would be fun. *Maybe I'll get laid, if they're not gay. Maybe I will anyway. Maybe I can do a* ménage à—

"Say Bill, Celia and I wonder if you're going to the Shark Feed," said Jennifer. We want to go but we're a little concerned. We'd like to have a strong dive buddy to hold onto if there's a problem. You look pretty strong."

"Right," said Celia, "Don told us it's fairly safe but we thought, you know, a group of three would offer more safety in numbers."

"Well I will certainly think about it." *Well, if that's what it takes . . .*

The women smiled sweetly, took off their bikini tops and jumped in the plunge pool. Bill joined them in a splashing, vodka-accelerated riot of fun.

After several days of diving in the lagoon the three became quite close. Bill slept one night with Celia and hoped that things would develop with Jennifer too—especially at the party after the Shark Feed. It was scheduled for later in the week. After that dive and showers, there would be drinks, along with a banquet and dancing. *A perfect opportunity to fulfill a fantasy!* Bill still hadn't decided whether he would go on the Shark Feed. But he was thinking that real men weren't afraid of fish. Jennifer, he'd speculated, liked real men.

●●●

The next day the divers took a walk. Beqa Island was formed from a volcano several million years ago. The island was lush with palm trees, ferns, banana plants and two small villages at different ends of the island. The natives were friendly, spoke English, and, to entertain visitors, walked on stones heated in an open fire. Their children charmed the divers with songs. That evening the divers had a ceremony with a local drink called Kava, which was a mild intoxicant. During the ceremony, and snookered somewhat on the Kava, Bill was selected as the *Ratu*, their tribal chief.

Don smiled. "That means, *Ratu,* that you lead us down to the Shark Feed."

Bill turned pale. "But I haven't decided to go."

He looked to Celia for support but she said, "Oh, *Ratu*, Jennifer and I thought you were going to be our dive buddy on that dive—and we'd planned a special treat for you afterwards."

Shit! Bill's mind raced. Fear fought with lust—and lost. *Maybe that treat is both of them.*

"Okay, I suppose it's safe. Right. I'll do it."

The day scheduled for the Shark Feed arrived. Bill elected to skip the early morning dive and stay on land to steel himself. He also wanted information about the sharks so he could impress the women. The lodge had an Internet connection and the home page had descriptions of the island and the lagoon. There were all kinds of animals, from fruit bats to mongoose to lizards on land. The sea life included dolphins, turtles, and shellfish. They'd already seen some neat octopuses on the previous dives. Bill was tempted to schedule a night dive. They had an entirely different array of sea life than a day dive. This was all interesting but he'd come for shark data. He googled "Bull Shark." Their size was consistent with Don's remarks:

> "Bull Sharks are large and stout. Males can reach 6.9 ft and weigh 198.4 lbs. Females can be much larger: 10.8 ft and 700 lbs. Bull Sharks are wider than other sharks of comparable length, and are grey on top and white below. The diet of a Bull Shark includes fish, other sharks, rays, dolphins, turtles, and even terrestrial mammals. Relatively calm Bull Sharks can suddenly become violent—"

What the hell? Bill began to wonder if the screwing he hoped to get would be worth the screwing he feared he'd get. These goddamn fish were terrifying. He did more searches. He learned that Bull sharks were in the same category as the Tiger and Great White sharks; they were the most aggressive species of sharks in the ocean. Further, they were territorial and the gang was going into their territory. *Damn.*

When Bill returned to his bungalow he found Jennifer waiting for him. "Jennifer, maybe we ought to rethink this Shark Feed."

"Bill, I don't want to talk about sharks. Let's take a swim and skip lunch. Celia tells me you're a great lover."

Bill's thinking apparatus suddenly shifted location and all thoughts of sharks disappeared as two hot intermingled bodies sank into his plunge pool.

●●●

That afternoon the divers boarded a boat and headed north to the Shark Feed location. As they tied onto a buoy they noticed three other boats headed for their position.

"Everyone in the water," commanded Don. "We want to be first at the right end of the wall where the sharks pass, after they grab their food."

The divers slapped on their gear, cranked open their air tanks and jumped en masse into the water. Don, carrying a huge video camera, and a reluctant *Ratu* Bill Casey, led the descent. On the bottom, they lined up behind the wall. Jennifer, Celia and Bill anchored the right end of the line. Soon the waters were filled with divers from the other boats—all assembled in linear fashion. Bill admitted to himself that the divers' air bubbles sure seemed like a wall.

He looked around. In front, and about twenty feet to his right, he saw a half-dozen Bull Sharks swimming in a tight circle. A Fiji dive master was in front of the wall—perhaps fifteen feet—with the chum bucket, and the diver was holding up small fish parts. A huge sphere-shaped ball of smaller fish was over the dive master's head. Fish dove and nibbled at the parts. Four handlers with long poles and a few spears were lined up behind the divers and two stood in front of the ends of the wall.

Every minute or so a Bull Shark would peel out of formation and sweep toward the chum bucket. It would be rewarded with a large fish head or carcass, perhaps from a Tuna, which it would snatch with enormous teeth, and then sweep along the wall passing within several feet of Bill and the women, to return to the waiting circle. It was awesome and Bill snorted in his mask—all the other divers were engaged in a photo-taking frenzy while the fish and sharks were in a feeding frenzy. There was so much food being delivered to the sharks that the ball of smaller fish wasn't threatened.

Don swam over and made a diver's "okay?" signal. Bill responded happily. This was working out and he had high expectations for a real treat back on land. Don pointed at his eyes and then himself, indicating that Bill and the women should watch him. He swam past the wall and planted himself just below the swirling sharks, turned on his camera and lights, and began filming the sharks from below. Just then, the ball of fish disintegrated—fish scattering in all directions. Then the Bull Sharks peeled off and left the area. Everyone looked around wondering what had happened. And then they saw it. A Tiger Shark, about fourteen feet long, had stumbled on the Shark Feed. Panic erupted. The guy feeding the fish scurried back to the wall. Bill and the girls looked over their shoulders. The handlers behind them had abandoned their posts. The handlers in front had dropped their spears and ducked behind the wall. Everyone looked at Don out there alone, with his camera. The Tiger looked at Don, too.

The Tiger is a solitary hunter, usually hunting at night. Its name is derived from dark stripes which run down its body. This was an adolescent since its stripes were pronounced; they fade as the shark ages. Tigers are dangerous predators—they'll eat anything. They've been found with metal and old tires in their stomach.

Don got as flat as he could. He held the camera in front and above him. The Tiger made a beeline for him and came swooping down. Bill Casey wanted to bolt for the boat but Celia, a more experienced diver, grabbed onto him and Jennifer. She signaled that they should stay together. Tigers, like lions hunting zebra, preferred to hunt a straggler or cut their prey out of the herd. As long as the herd stayed together it was relatively safe. But Don was on his own.

Bill began to worry about his air. It was in short supply. They'd been at fifty feet depth for over forty-five minutes. They had to make a decompression stop at fifteen feet, for five minutes. If they couldn't get to fifteen feet they were in for more trouble. Even if the shark let them race for the surface they might get the bends. No single diver could use the air tanks, hanging under the boats, with the Tiger prowling the area. Further, Bill was getting cold.

Don, on the other hand, was sweating. The Tiger came right at him and he couldn't move.

As the Tiger dropped down on Don, he jammed the camera up. The shark dropped and ground its body into Don. The other divers gasped as Don's entire body seemed to disappear under the Tiger. Bill wondered how they were going to get back to their boats with this predator in the water.

Bill knew, from his Internet research, that only the Great White sharks were responsible for more human deaths than Tigers. He watched as Don stared up into a bright yellow underbelly of the twisting Tiger. Bill figured this shark weighed about seven hundred fifty pounds. He was ready to abandon hope for Don when the Tiger abruptly called off its attack and swam away. Don was halfway back to the wall when the fish returned; it had made a one hundred eighty degree turn and was coming back again. It was fast, too. Tigers can go twenty miles per hour, faster in a burst. This time it passed over the wall, right through that so-called impenetrable wall of rising bubbles, and terrified every single diver. Playing coy again, it swam out and turned and charged on Don again, who had reached the wall. With his back to the wall, and his legs and rump on the floor, Don took the full brunt of the charge, once more jamming the camera into the bottom of the shark's mouth. Enraged, the Tiger twisted and ground down but could make no headway.

As the Tiger pulled away in frustration, some of the handlers herded a bunch of divers up to the decompression tanks. Keeping a reef to their back and hanging on each others' arms to maintain a compact ball, the divers took their five minutes of air while the Tiger circled endlessly. When the shark made another exit pass they scampered up to their boats and another bunch wormed their way up to the tanks. Bill Casey reached the extra air tanks with a few minutes left in his tank. The women, who use less air, had about ten minutes.

On the boat returning to Beqa Island, Bill asked Don what he'd been thinking during the attack. "I thought about crocodiles and how they have tremendous compression strength in their jaws, but very little extension strength. I figured maybe sharks were the same and I rammed the camera up to keep its mouth from opening. I guess I was right." Then Don excused himself, walked to the rail, and disgorged a mighty trail of vomit.

That night, in addition to some long, hot showers, there were a lot of wet suits thrown in the lodge washing machines—with extra detergents. Still, divers are a hearty bunch, and by the time the banquet was over the Tiger had grown another three feet. Later, dancing with Celia and Jennifer, Bill felt a rush of adrenaline explode in his system. By the time the women got him to his bungalow, he was unconscious, from all the excitement. Bill didn't get his *ménage à trois*.

●●●

One year later, Don's Dive Shop organized its next trip to Fiji. En route, Bill Casey, by now an experienced diver with fifty dives, was sitting next to Stan, a new diver from Los Angeles.

"Tell me, Stan, are you coming to the Shark Feed on this trip?"

"Shark Feed? No one told me about a Shark Feed. Is it included in the price?"

"It's just an extra hundred bucks and it's worth every penny."

"Ain't it dangerous?"

"Not at all," said Celia, seated behind Bill.

"It's a kick," said Jennifer.

Bill looked at Stan and smiled.

Big Numbers Are Larger Than Small Numbers

Professor Karl Menger walked out of the Federal Express office on El Camino Real in Mountain View, California. A Black BMW 330i, racing a red 1961 Porsche 356, caught his attention. He gasped as the BMW ran down a little boy on a bicycle. As the cars sped away the professor recognized some of the digits on the license plate of the BMW. Menger reached into his jacket, grabbed his cell phone, and dialed 911. A few moments later, the scene was engulfed in police cars and an ambulance.

"So, your name is Karl Menger? You're a professor at Stanford. Is that correct?" asked the policeman.

"Yes officer, I saw the whole thing. *Es war schechlich*. Excuse me, it was terrible. The poor little boy—"

"On the 911 call, you said you saw some of the numbers on the license plate. Is that correct?"

"Yes, *der Schwein*. It was a California license plate, and I saw the numbers 2-7-1-8. There were some other numbers, before and after, but I don't remember them."

"Well, thank you, Professor. Someone from the District Attorney's office will be in touch."

•••

A few weeks later, the police arrested Mr. John Baptista, a wealthy businessman of Portuguese descent, from Macao, residing in Los Altos, California, for hit and run and assault with a deadly weapon. Mr. Baptista posted a huge bond, and trial was set for December 15.

•••

Judge Shirley Juarez called the court to order. Representing the people was ADA Jack Webster; defense counsel was Ms. Susan Lohse, Esq., from the firm of Schwartz and Carruthers. The prosecution began its case and, after introducing considerable evidence implicating Mr. Baptista, Mr. Webster called Professor Menger as a witness for the people.

Professor Menger was sworn—although there was some confusion in the courtroom over his reluctance to swear on a bible. This was due, in part, to his penchant for speaking German. In the trial transcript, the translator explained that the professor, when asked to swear on the bible, engaged in an internal, but audible, debate in German with himself, as to whether God was an integer, or simply any kind of number.

Judge Juarez, herself not an expert on the distinction between integers and other numbers, nor, for that matter, an expert on anything involving numbers, instructed Professor Menger to concentrate on the issues, and to speak in English. She concluded, "Now, Professor Menger. Let me explain something. As you can see we do not have a jury. That's because this is a bench trial. I am the sole arbitrator; in simplistic terms, I'm the finder of fact. I'll be the one that determines whether Mr. Baptista is innocent or guilty. Do you understand?"

● ● ●

[Court Reporter's Note: Partial Trial Transcript Follows]

Professor Menger:	Yes, Your Honor.
Judge Juarez:	Okay Mr. Webster, you can continue.
Mr. Webster:	Good morning, Professor. You're a mathematician?
Professor Menger:	That's correct. I hold a PhD in mathematics from the University of Heidelberg; and I am professor of mathematics at Stanford University.
Mr. Webster:	Did you see an automobile accident at 12:30 PM, on the 11th of October, on El Camino Real in Mountain View, California?
Professor Menger:	I saw a black BMW 330i run down a little boy on a bicycle.
Mr. Webster:	How did you know it was a BMW?
Professor Menger:	I am German, of course, and therefore quite familiar with BMWs.
Mr. Webster:	Yes! Thank you. Now, according to the police report, which is the people's exhibit number twelve, you told the police the car that hit the little boy had a California license plate, and that the first five digits were 9-2-7-1-8. Is that correct?
Professor Menger:	No. I told the police that I saw the digits 2-7-1-8. I believe they followed the first digit. I do not

	remember the first digit. I don't know where the nine came from.
Mr. Webster:	Now, Professor Menger, why is it you did not notice the first digit, but it is that you noticed the next four digits?
Professor Menger:	That's quite easy to explain, you see; those four digits I noticed are the first four digits of a famous transcendental irrational number, known as *e*, the base of natural logarithms. *Ich habe, entschuldigung* . . . [Translator's note: *lit.* I have, excuse me . . .] I have used it often as a combination for hotel safes.

●●●

Professor Menger thought fondly back to his days at the University of Heidelberg. In those days many Germans with a safe chose Adolf Hitler's birthday as their combination; April 20, 1889, for example, 2-0-4-8-9. But not the professor; he chose an irrational number.

Interrupting the professor's reverie, Mr. Webster asked, "And what, sir, is an irrational number? Could you explain it to the judge? What did you call it? '*e*'?"

●●●

[Court Reporter's Note: Partial Trial Transcript Follows]

Professor Menger:	Yes. *e* is an irrational number whose digits never repeat and continue forever.
Ms. Lohse:	I object. Is the professor telling us that the number goes on forever?
Judge Juarez:	I think that's what he said. Excuse me, Professor. Did you say forever?
Professor Menger:	Yes, Your Honor, it is infinitely long. The first 8 digits are 2 *point* 7-1-8-2-8-1-8. I am afraid I cannot memorize the rest. That would be impossible.
Judge Juarez:	Well Ms. Lohse, that's his answer. We'll note your objection for the record. During cross you may challenge this testimony. Off the record.

I'm looking forward to that. [Court Reporter's Note: Redacted]

Judge Juarez:	Back on the Record. Mr. Webster?

Mr. Webster:	Yes, thank you, Your Honor. And thank you, Professor. Your Honor, the people have no further questions for this witness.
Judge Juarez:	Your witness, Ms. Lohse.
Ms. Lohse:	Good morning, Professor. Any chance you saw the rest of the number?
Professor Menger:	I don't understand. Do you mean the rest of e? That's not possible?
Ms. Lohse:	Well, I thought you said that you saw eeeh on the plate. Didn't you?
Mr. Webster:	Your Honor? Really! The defense should pay attention to the answers. If the court reporter checks the record, he can show the court that the eminent Professor said he only saw the first four digits of e.
Judge Juarez:	Please, Mr. Webster, let's let the court reporter stick his own transcript in his mouth. Ms. Lohse, you may continue.
Ms. Lohse:	I'm very sorry I was confused, Your Honor. Yes, I understand now that he saw the first four digits of eeeh. Professor, I meant to ask you if you saw any numbers after the first four digits on the license plate.
Professor Menger:	I am not a lawyer and please, Your Honor, don't get mad at me, but may I correct the question? I think Ms. Lohse wants to know if I saw any digits on the license plate *after* the first four digits of e which were the second to the fifth digits on the license plate. *Nicht wahr,* [Translator's note: *lit.* Not True? *id.* Is that right?] Ms. Lohse?
Ms. Lohse:	Professor Menger, you give the answers, and in English, if you please. We get to ask the questions. That's how American jurisprudence works. Please answer your own question.
Professor Menger:	No, I don't remember any more digits.
Ms. Lohse:	Professor, I need to get a better understanding of this, what did you call it, an irrational number? It's hard for me to understand how something irrational can be used to convict my client. Can you give the court another example of such an irrational number?

●●●

The professor found the question curious. There were more irrational numbers than rational numbers, but he suspected that his audience might have problems understanding that concept. He decided to keep it simple. A circle, he thought, was a pretty simple shape.

● ● ●

[Court Reporter's Note: Partial Trial Transcript Follows]

Professor Menger:	Well, there's *pi*. You would know it as the ratio of a circle's circumference to its diameter.
Ms. Lohse:	Are you also telling the court that this number; pie as you called it, also goes on forever? For a circle that any third grader could draw, with a compass and a pencil?
Dr. Menger:	Yes, it would go on forever. It's an irrational number.
Ms. Lohse:	Let's stay with this pie thing. Now if I draw, a circle that's half the size, or, for that matter, twice the size, of the first circle, would I get the same pie?
Professor Menger:	*Vorsicht!* [Translator's note: *lit.* (1) Caution! (2) Danger!] You are straying into dangerous territory, Ms. Lohse. You're about to introduce another irrational number called the square root of two. Further, a doubled, or halved circle, cannot be constructed with a pencil and a compass. That's called 'squaring the circle' and it is not possible. Even the ancient Greeks knew this although it was not proven until 1882. *Man soll den schlafenden Löwen nicht wecken.* [Translator's note: *id.* Let sleeping dogs lie.]
Ms. Lohse:	I suppose you'll tell us that the square root of two goes on forever too. Does it?
Professor Menger:	Yes, it goes on forever.
Ms. Lohse:	And what about those circles? Are all their pies the same and do they go on forever?
Professor Menger:	Well, *pi* is the same for all circles but, actually, it goes on forever and forever.
Ms. Lohse:	Don't you mean just forever?
Professor Menger:	I meant one forever for the square root of two. But I mean forever and forever for *pi*. You see, there are some forevers that are longer than other forevers. You might want to study Cantor; he showed there is a whole class of forevers, which he called infinities.

●●●

Ms. Lohse was secretly thrilled. The Professor had fallen into a trap. She could not believe how lucky she that Professor Menger had inadvertently picked *pi* as an example of another so-called irrational number. Still, she wasn't ready to spring the trap, so she continued her ruse with pie.

●●●

[Court Reporter's Note: Partial Trial Transcript Follows]

Ms. Lohse:	Well, we're going to see about that forever and forever thing for pie. But, for now, let's see if I can understand this infinity thing with a simple case. Suppose I start multiplying one times one times one, and so forth, an infinite number of times. Doesn't that always result in one?
Professor Menger:	Yes, you will end up at one, unless, of course, you make a mistake in the multiplication. But it will take you forever to get to one.
Ms. Lohse:	But isn't one a rational number?
Professor Menger:	Yes.
Ms. Lohse:	Your Honor, how can it take forever? This is not rational.
Judge Juarez:	Well, he did say that some things are irrational. However I must admit that I am puzzled.

●●●

The Judge wondered how one could make a mistake multiplying one times one times one and so forth. Judge Juarez started to carry out the arithmetic on her note pad. Unfortunately the Judge had a sloppy handwriting style and, by the third multiplication, she wrote down eleven instead of one, which, after several more iterations, led to one hundred twenty-one. She thought this was more complicated than it seemed.

●●●

[Court Reporter's Note: Partial Trial Transcript Follows]

Ms. Lohse:	This is absurd, Professor. Let's go back to this infinity thing. You say it would also take forever to list all of its digits? Correct?

Professor Menger:	Yes, it would take one forever.
Ms. Lohse:	I'm confused, Professor. Did you say "one forever?" But the digits are not all ones, are they?
Professor Menger:	Good heavens, no.
Ms. Lohse:	Well, bear with me a little. How do you know when you've accounted for all the digits in infinity?
Professor Menger:	That's quite simple. We line them up with the integers, for example, one, two, three, and so forth. Or, if you prefer, we could use the even or odd integers or even the squares.
Ms. Lohse:	And what about pie? If we lined the digits up with the integers, would it also take forever?
Professor Menger:	I believe I said it would take two forevers for *pi*.
Judge Juarez:	Excuse me, Ms. Lohse. I have a question for the witness. Professor Menger, What if I use one of your suggestions, such as the squares of the integers, like one, four, nine, and so forth? Wouldn't that get me there sooner?
Dr. Menger:	I am sad to say, Your Honor, that it still would take two forevers to list all the digits in *pi*. One can place the digits of that pesky square root of two, in a one-to-one correspondence with the integers, or, just the even or odd integers, or even their squares, as you inquired. But the use of the squares would still take forever. And it would take two of those forevers for *pi*.

● ● ●

Her trap sprung, Ms. Lohse went for the jugular! The professor had clearly committed himself to the preposterous notion that *pi* went on forever and ever. Grabbing tables of the digits of *e* and *pi* and waving them in the air, Ms. Lohse returned to the circus.

● ● ●

[Court Reporter's Note: Partial Trial Transcript Follows]

Ms Lohse:	Well, Professor, I'm afraid I've got you. Your Honor, I can prove that *pi* does not go on forever. I have precedent. The General Assembly of the state of Indiana, in 1897, passed a bill unanimously—in point of fact 67-to-0—declaring that *pi* was a constant 3.2.

	That doesn't sound to me like a number that goes on forever. It's true that the Indiana state Senate has yet to ratify the pending bill, so it's not black letter law; but it demonstrates legislative intent. They even publish tables of these numbers.
Professor Menger:	*Gott im Himmel.* [Translator's note: *lit.* God in Heaven. *id.* My God!] I think you don't understand. As I have already explained these numbers are infinitely long. One needs an infinite series to define them. And if I might add, the General Assembly of the state of Indiana is populated by *arselochen*! [Translator's note: Expletive not translated.]
Judge Juarez:	Professor Menger. Please watch your language. I don't know what it meant but it sounded crude. These are solemn proceedings. I must admonish you to answer only the question that you're asked. Mr. Webster, it looks to me like your witness is imploding.
Mr. Webster:	Perhaps not, Your Honor. I think Ms. Lohse is wrong. There's got to be some reason the state of Indiana Senate hasn't ratified that bill in one hundred eleven years. I would like to ask the court to line up the digits of *pi* with the integers. Perhaps we could work right through lunch to settle this 3.2 thing once and for all. My case rests on showing that Dr. Menger recognized some of the digits of *e* on Mr. Baptista's license plate; his credibility is paramount.
Judge Juarez:	Alright. Ms. Lohse, considering this is a felonious assault charge; I'm willing to grant the prosecution some leeway. However, I think we can accelerate the process. With everyone's agreement, perhaps we could use the squares of the integers.
Mr. Webster:	Yes, Your Honor. I am very interested in seeing what happens when we get to 3.2; so, by all means let's get there faster.
Judge Juarez:	Good. Clearly, big numbers are larger than small numbers and I'm getting hungry. Let's see, if the court reporter can start lining up the digits of *pi*; I think we line up one squared or one, with three; two squared or four, with one; three squared or nine, with four; four squared … did I get that right, Professor?
Professor Menger:	Well, pi does start with 3 *point* 1-4-1-5-9, but I am sorry, Your Honor. This process will take more than

	our lifetimes to work. You can try to line up the digits of *pi* with the squares of the integers; but it will not get you to *pi* any sooner. And I can assure you we will never, ever, get to 3.2.
Ms. Lohse:	Well, it can't take long to further discredit the People's witness, Your Honor. With your permission, let's ask the reporter to start at the one millionth digit of *pi*. It shouldn't take too long that way.
Judge Juarez:	All right, lunch can wait. Professor, please remain in your seat. You have not been dismissed. The court reporter will start with the one millionth digit of *pi* and the square of one million and keep lining them up.
Dr. Menger:	Your Honor, this is *verruckt*. [Translator's note: *lit.* crazy.] We will be here forever. *Sie sollen alles 'rausgeschmissen werden. Der Taten finden, mein füss*! [Translator's note: *id.* You should all get the ax! *lit.* Find the facts, my foot!]
Judge Juarez:	Well, Professor, we all know you think forever is really forever, although some of your forevers might be longer than others. But, for the purposes of judicial efficiency, let's start even higher, say, at the one billionth digit. Go on, Mr. Reporter. We haven't got all day.
Court Reporter:	All right Your Honor. From page 936,037 of the court's reference tables, the one billionth digit of pi is . . .

●●●

The Superior Court of the County of Santa Clara is still in session. When the court reporter reached the one billion two-thousand thirteenth digit of *pi*, Mr. Baptista snuck out of the courtroom. He took a taxi to San Francisco International Airport and flew to Hong Kong on Cathay Pacific Airlines, using his brother's passport. He was last seen entering the Macao Ferry Building in the Central District of Hong Kong. Professor Menger expired on the stand shortly thereafter, from a ruptured bladder.

Data

The voters of the state of California adopted an amendment to Proposition Thirteen that changed the property tax regulations for the first time in twenty-five years. This amendment provided for the taxation of data bases on commercial computer systems. Software applications and programs were exempt from the new tax.

The county of Santa Clara leapt at the opportunity to increase its tax base. The data base of IGF Credit DB Systems, Inc., a company that monitored credit data on fifteen million Americans, was assessed a value of $100 Million by the County Tax Assessment Board. This yielded a tax of $3.2 Million. IGF appealed the assessment on the grounds that the law was unconstitutionally vague, and offered no guidance to the public as to how to enforce it. Despite its appeal, IGF was obligated to pay the tax in advance. The appeal was underway in the California State Court of Tax Appeals.

$$\bullet\bullet\bullet$$

In the matter of the IGF Credit DB Systems, Inc. v. County of Santa Clara Tax Assessor: Case number A-2006-0001-33.

Judge Henry B. Winston,	Senior Appellate Judge, Presiding
The County of Santa Clara:	Mr. Stanley Braidman
For IGF Credit:	Ms. Susan Lohse, Carruthers and Schwartz

$$\bullet\bullet\bullet$$

Ms. Lohse:	We'd like to call an expert witness on software, Your Honor.
Judge Winston:	What will this expert testify about, Ms. Lohse?
Ms. Lohse:	Your Honor, the tax bill provides for a tax on data and not on programs. We intend to show that data and programs are indistinguishable; that programs are data, and that data are programs. We have a distinguished expert to attest to these facts. After the

	expert's testimony, I'm confident the court will find for the appellant and refund the $3.2 Million.
Mr. Braidman:	Your Honor, relevance? I object. This is absurd. Everyone knows that data are different from programs.
Judge Whinston:	Well, let's hear the expert's credentials. Personally I don't know what a program is. Perhaps this is relevant. Motion denied. Go ahead, Ms. Lohse, introduce your expert.
Ms. Lohse:	I call Peter K. Lemming.

● ● ●

Peter Lemming took the stand. He was a diminutive man, about fifty-five years old, with graying hair and a large nose. He looked confidently at Ms. Lohse, straightened his tie and cleared his throat in a professorial manner.

● ● ●

Ms. Lohse:	So, Mr. Lemming. Would you please state your credentials in computers and software?
Mr. Lemming:	Certainly, I have a PhD from the University of Washington in computer science, I did a post doc at Georgetown and I'm vice president and director of computing research at Menlo Defense Research Institute, where I manage one hundred seventy-five people, many with PhDs. I've published professionally in refereed journals, of course. I started programming in 1968 which makes me a pioneer in computing. I've received the Distinguished Service Award from the Association for Software Systems (ASS). Most recently I was invited to speak on the Internet to the Boy Scouts of America.
Ms. Lohse:	Are those sufficient credentials, Your Honor, to satisfy the court and qualify Dr. Lemming as an expert in this matter?
Judge Whinston:	It seems adequate to me although I thought the modern day of computing began in World War II, which would make him a second generation pioneer. Mr. Braidman?
Mr. Braidman:	I'd call him something else. But no, I have no questions, Your Honor. I'll wait for cross.
Judge Whinston:	All right Ms. Lohse, Dr. Lemming is accepted as an expert in software.

Ms. Lohse:	Thank you, Your Honor. Now, Dr. Lemming, can you explain what software is?
Dr. Lemming:	Certainly. Software is what turns a general purpose computer into a special purpose problem solving machine. It tells the machine what to do.
Ms. Lohse:	Well, aren't computers smarter than us? Don't they know what to do?
Dr. Lemming:	No, actually they're intellectual morons, incapable of original thought. They need to be told precisely what to do.
Ms Lohse:	I see. Now, what is a program?
Dr. Lemming:	A program is a precise list of instructions to the machine which tells it what to do.
Ms. Lohse:	Could you give the court an example?
Dr. Lemming:	Sure, like *store* or *multiply*.
Ms. Lohse:	Surely computers can do more than that Dr. Lemming. True?
Dr. Lemming:	Well I was being simplistic, but actually at the most basic level, they can only add, shift, test for one or zero, and read or write.
Ms. Lohse:	So how do computers do all that fancy stuff?
Dr. Lemming:	They string together all those adds, shifts, and so forth in long, very long, programs.
Ms. Lohse:	Okay, so what're data to a computer?
Dr. Lemming:	Data are things programs work with to get answers.
Ms. Lohse:	Suppose I want to write a program. What do I do first?
Dr. Lemming:	Well, you write your program and submit it as data to another program which turns it into a machine language program—something the machine can understand in bits and bytes. We call that an object program.
Judge Whinston:	Wait a minute, Ms. Lohse. Sorry to interrupt. Dr. Lemming, if I may ask, that second program you mentioned? It treats the first program as data? How can that be? And it produces a third program?
Dr. Lemming:	Well, you see, sometimes programs are data, and sometimes data are programs. We have other programs called operating systems that manage all this for us. Programs are data to operating systems.
Ms. Lohse:	You see Your Honor. *Res ipsa loquitor*; it speaks for itself. It's all the same. Programs are data.
Judge Whinston:	I didn't hear it speak, Ms. Lohse. Maybe they're the same, but I can't keep up with all these programs. I

need some clarification. Now, Dr. Lemming, I believe you said operating systems are programs. How do they become programs? Do they start as data, and then grow into programs?

Dr. Lemming: Your Honor, I know it's confusing, sometimes even to me, and I'm a former president of the Association of Software Systems. The answer is those operating systems are data to other programs in one, or another, operating system.

Judge Whinston: And can you mix data and programs together? How do you know which is which?

Dr. Lemming: Yes, even though we think of them as different, they're mixed together quite frequently. Dr. von Neumann would say that programs and data differ only by the manner in which they're interpreted, at the time that the central processor looks at them.

Judge Whinston: What's a central processor?

Dr. Lemming: That's the computer's brain, Your Honor.

Judge Whinston: Thank you. Ms. Lohse? Are you finished? At this point in the proceedings, I think it would be useful to let Mr. Braidman ask some questions. I will allow you to continue your inquiry later, if necessary. We can always cut and paste the transcript during adjudication. Mr. Braidman? The county looks like it's in a big hole now. How can it tax one, and not the other?

Mr. Braidman: Your Honor, I can't keep up with all this tautology. However, before the county concedes, we have a long way to go. First, I'd like to review the expert's credentials.

Ms. Lohse: I object. The court has already accepted this witness as an expert.

Judge Whinston: Mr. Braidman?

Mr. Braidman: Yes, Your Honor. It is unusual to reopen that issue—but the witness has opened the door with his own words.

Judge Whinston: Yes, I suppose he's used some strange words. The motion is denied. But let's keep it handy. Alright, Mr. Braidman, please proceed.

Mr. Braidman: Thank you. Now, Dr. Lemming, I believe you said you're the vice president and director of computing research at Menlo Defense Research Institute. Is that correct?

Dr. Lemming:	Yes. I manage all research in computing.
Mr. Braidman:	And are you being paid for today's testimony?
Dr. Lemming:	No, Carruthers and Schwartz is paying MDRI directly for my time. I only receive my normal salary, and a small stipend; an honorarium, to compensate for my time under oath.
Mr. Braidman:	You mean you get a bonus for telling the truth?
Dr. Lemming:	Please, sir. I always tell the truth.
Mr. Braidman:	Uh-huh. That's comforting. Well, let's go back to your research. What subjects do you study?
Dr. Lemming:	We do research in theoretical computer science, robotics, artificial intelligence, and telecommunications.
Mr. Braidman:	Did you say artificial intelligence?
Dr. Lemming:	Yes, I did and we are very proud of our new AI laboratory.
Mr. Braidman:	I see. Well, I won't ask where you got the funding for that laboratory. And what is AI?
Ms. Lohse:	Your Honor! This is outrageous. Where does Mr. Braidman think they got the funding?
Judge Whinston:	Relax, Ms. Lohse. I don't care where they got the money and I'm the only one that counts. Mr. Court Reporter, please repeat Mr. Braidman's question.
Court Reporter:	And what is AI?
Dr. Lemming:	We teach machines how to think. You know, things like recognize natural language and act like experts in certain fields.
Mr. Braidman:	You teach the computer's brain, the central processor like you mentioned earlier? Is that what you mean?
Dr. Lemming:	Well, sort of. We give the machine a program which shows it how to think. And we give it data to assist the program.
Mr. Braidman:	But Dr. Lemming, didn't you say that computers can't think for themselves. That they're intellectual morons in your own words? Which is it, Dr. Lemming? You can't have it both ways. Can't the machine think without that data you have to give it?
Dr. Lemming:	I object Your Honor. He's twisted my words.
Judge Whinston:	You can't object, Dr. Lemming. You're the witness. Ms. Lohse, I was inclined to rule in your favor but this witness is clearly unreliable. First he said that machines can't think. Then he said programs and data are the same. Then he said machines can think

but they need data which is different from the thinker part. In the presence of doubt I must rule for the county.

Mr. Braidman: Thank you, Your Honor. I move for an immediate dismissal of the appeal, letting the tax assessment and payment stand.

Judge Whinston: So ordered! Court adjourned.

That Room

We stood there like sheep lined up. My God, we'd paid a premium to get a turn. There had been a feeding frenzy to get the tickets. "Come early," we'd been told, and every fifteen minutes the attendants shepherded out an old batch of *candidates* and ushered in a new batch—into that room. The people who came out were pale, with glazed eyes, and some limped.

Yesterday I'd watched the process unfold at the Maui Writers' conference in the Wailea Marriott. Four batches an hour, six hours a day, and ten candidates a batch—two hundred forty people a day—went into that room and came out—different. Was it an alien plot to take over the world—like *The Invasion of the Body Snatchers*? They were only in there ten minutes, yet some seemed older on their way out.

I swore some of the candidates had puncture wounds on their throats. And more eerily, some seemed smaller—could it have been an odorless gas that had affected them, such as in the manner of *The Incredible Shrinking Man*? Not too many people looked happy; just a few sported malevolent grins. Their eyes, I'd thought, had flashed with greed, and their teeth looked longer than normal.

Those of us in line for the 9:15 AM session were nervous. I sensed that most were going into that room for the first time—except for one man who came out of the 9:00 AM session and got back in line. We tried to get some information, some feedback, from the experienced ones as they trickled out, but they shunned us. Most were grim. The rest were in a weird fugue, with distant and weak smiles on their faces. The one repeat offender was shaky.

A bell rang! I thought a siren, like the one in *The Time Machine,* would have been more appropriate. But it sounded like Tinker Bell. The attendants opened the doors and we went to our assigned tables. I looked at the woman seated at my table. An Interrogator? Master? Agent? Teacher? I wasn't sure. I wondered if she thought me a sycophant, a student, or a victim. I looked into her eyes. Fantastic. She was beautiful. Stunning! Magnificent. It wasn't human to be that attractive. I tried to talk. I felt myself sinking, as though someone had deflated a raft and I was going to drown. Time stood still; time raced. The next thing I knew I was outside that room. I had a piece of paper in my hand—but I was too confused to read it. I could barely breathe. I was weak; I couldn't remember what had been said. Had she said something good or bad? Was I wounded? Was my life changed? I jammed the note in my pocket. The people in the next batch looked at me. "What happened in there?" asked one of them. I answered that I didn't know. But I felt like I'd lost a pint of blood.

Meanwhile, the assembly line continued to process more people. Henry Ford would have been proud. At forty dollars a slot, $9600 was changing hands daily—and the humans were doing it voluntarily. Someone was eating well; could some of it have been human flesh? I looked at my arms but there were no bite marks.

Frustrated, I decided to try again. Yes, bizarre as that sounds, I decided that I had to know what had happened in that room. I paid my blood money; stood in another line, and kept my silence—I didn't want to alarm the others in the new batch. These days poorly chosen words can spark a riot. The conference was crowded and someone could have been crushed or hurt.

Tinker Bell tinkled and I took my assigned seat. Another woman—Mentor? Superior? Leader? Docent?—she was gorgeous, too. But this time, I controlled myself. I looked down and sideways. I allowed myself limited eye contact, fearful that I might sink once more into a bottomless pit. I took notes—*I thought*. I listened. But when Tinker Bell rang again, I was still confused. Outside, I wondered what had happened in that room. None of the other candidates were smiling? Why was I smiling? I had another piece of paper in my hand. It had some writing on it. I reached into my pocket and retrieved the earlier note. Both notes were in other peoples' handwriting. Both had sweat drop stains. Was that blood or fingernail polish on the corner of one? My eyes blurred, my glasses fogged. I scurried into a corner and took a deep breath. Then I rubbed my eyes, wiped off my glasses, and studied the notes.

Both notes said "send a proposal." Both had email addresses. My God, I'd done it! I'd survived the *Pitch Room* intact. It was time for a cigar and a seventeen-year-old single malt Scotch whisky. No rejection! A publisher and an agent had both requested the very same book proposal.

Top Secret

Mao Zedong launched the Cultural Revolution that day in 1966, and the United States government was concerned. It was not a good time to ask the government to share its secrets.

Agent Cararro, who was with the Defense Investigative Service (DIS), straightened his narrow tie, withdrew several documents from his portfolio—one of those leather ones with the words Department of Defense stamped on its side—and gave me a curious look. We sat in the conference room of the Security Office at Menlo Defense Research Institute (MDRI) where I led a team of experts in electronic warfare. The room had a beat-up old wooden conference table, dirty beige walls, and fluorescent lighting that hissed and popped occasionally. It was cold, too.

"So, Mr. Meades, you're applying for top secret clearance?"

"I need access; some of my team's projects could operate at a higher funding level if the application is approved." I admit I was nervous. It was my first clearance application at that level and I worried how they would deal with my family secret, if they ever found out. There was risk too, if I didn't get access they could lift my existing secret clearance. That would kill my job at MDRI.

"I see," said Cararro. He had a slight sneer. "It must be nice to get government money."

I suspected the man was hostile to the application. It probably went with the job. I decided not to give him any unnecessary information. I waited for his questions.

"Mr. Meades, a top secret clearance requires that we investigate your complete background. We're going to review your past, including your education, friends and family, employment, and present and past residences. Let's review your Personnel Security Questionnaire."

The questionnaire was a multi-page government form several feet long. The government wanted information including your date of birth, draft board number, your address as well as previous residences for the past seventeen years, and the schools attended. I wondered what civil libertarians thought of the document that also demanded your arrest records, memberships in any organizations, parentage, personal references, race, and whether any relatives were living outside the country. The government even wanted to know if your spouse had foreign relatives. The appendix listed hundreds of organizations designated by the attorney general, and pursuant to Executive Order 10450, as Totalitarian, Fascist, Communist, or Subversive, or as having adopted a policy of advocating or approving the commission of acts of force and violence to deny others their rights under the Constitution of the United States, or which sought to alter the form of Government of the United States by unconstitutional means. This included such expected organizations as the Communist Party U.S.A., as well as some surprises like the Committee for the Negro in the Arts, the Congress of American Revolutionary Writers, and the Sakura Kai—Patriotic Society or Cherry Association and composed of veterans of the Russo-Japanese war. You had to certify that you were not now, and had never been a member of such organizations.

Cararro looked over my completed form, folded it, and dropped it in his portfolio. Then he turned on a bright desk lamp, swiveled it around, and pointed it in my face.

"We know that you received an earlier lower level secret clearance, granted when you joined the Air National Guard in 1956. Was the application that you completed in 1956 truthful and complete? Would you like to change any of your answers?" The questions flew out of his mouth like bullets from an automatic weapon.

"I have no changes. The answers were complete. Everything I said at that time was true." I'd decided to hedge a little, confident that the intent of my answers in 1956 had been truthful and, after all, I hadn't known the family secret then.

"Then let's get down to business." He walked me through the form and double checked all of my answers. Yes, my National Guard discharge had been Honorable and yes, I'd belonged to the Boy Scouts of America at a time when they'd worn brown shirts—didn't they still wear brown shirts? Yes, I'd belonged to an investment club that had purchased stock in K-Mart, apparently a suspect act.

"Do you object to us contacting your former neighbors?"

"No," I replied grudgingly. I could picture them saying "He must be a Commie" after being visited by an investigator.

"Mr. Meades, let's talk about your organizations. Do you now, or have you ever, belonged to an organization that advocates the violent overthrow of the Constitution of the United States?"

"Please, sir," I said a little irritated. "I have never belonged to any such organization. We've already checked those questions on the form."

"Thank you. However questions seventeen through twenty-one are quite specific. I'd like to review them again. Of course, none of this would be necessary—if you'd volunteer for a polygraph examination." He turned his head up, at an angle and raised his eyebrows in an inquisitive and hungry manner.

I had visions of an electric chair in a 1930's movie. I shook my head. Hoping that it sounded indifferent, I said, "Perhaps, Mr. Cararro, but I've never taken a lie detector test, and I'd like to get some advice first."

"You mean a lawyer, talk to a lawyer, don't you?"

"Perhaps. Why don't you ask your specific questions?" I hoped to steer him away from the polygraph and the lawyer issue.

"All right, Mr. Meades. Are you now or have you ever been—?"

After a while, we completed the same questions and I felt that I'd done well. He looked as though he were satisfied and began to stow the rest of his documents.

"That's very nice, Mr. Meades. You've convinced me that you're a loyal American. That's not easy to do. We'll be in touch about the background investigation with the neighbors and the like."

I smiled with relief as he grabbed his portfolio and rose from his chair.

"Oh, one last question," he said, "if you don't mind." He'd been headed toward the door but turned. He pulled a card out of his pocket which he proceeded to read. "Do you know anyone that has ever been a member of any foreign or domestic organization, association, movement, group, or combination of persons which is Totalitarian, Fascist, Communist, or Subversive, or which has adopted or shows a policy of advocating or approving the commission of acts of force or violence to deny other persons their rights under the Constitution of the United States?" His emphasis was on the words *know anyone*.

I gulped. Was it possible they knew my nasty little secret, the one I'd only learned about last year?

"Er, well," I mumbled, "Does it really matter these days? You're already convinced I'm a loyal American and that I never belonged to any such organizations."

Cararro returned to his chair. He looked at me suspiciously. "Cut the crap, Mr. Meades. Do you know anyone? Your 1956 application states quite clearly that you did not. Were you lying then or are you . . . Well you know the question. Do you know anyone that belonged to those organizations?"

I took a deep breath and looked out the window. Horses were grazing in the hills off of Sand Hill Road. I wished I were one of them. I figured my job was toast, nodded my head, and whimpered, "Yes, I did know one person that belonged to such an organization."

"Which organization would that be, Mr. Meades?"

"Is this really necessary? Is this legal? Do I have to tell you?"

"What's that you asked, Mr Meades? Did you say legal?"

"Do I really have to say?"

"Mr. Meades!!"

I tried to talk but no sounds came out of my mouth. Then, I steeled myself and managed to mutter, "Communist, the Communist Party U.S.A."

He squinted. I suspected he was anticipating the promotion he'd earn for nailing a Red.

"Who was this person?"

I bleated out, "My mother."

"Your mother was a Commie?" He was on the edge of his seat. "She carried a card. When? For how long? When did you know? Did you know in 1956? Did you lie on that application? Are you a Communist, too?" That automatic was firing again.

The questions were overwhelming. I was innocent; I had answers, but I felt hopeless. Growing up in the McCarthy era had conditioned everyone I knew to shun Communists—it would have been too dangerous to associate with them. Once tainted, you were a goner. I stared at Agent Cararro for a while.

"Look," I admitted, "my mother was a Communist but she quit the party when they assassinated Trotsky. That was 1943. She was a theoretical Communist; Stalin was too brutal. I was five years old at the time, so I wasn't much of a Communist. When I completed that form in 1956 I didn't know she'd been in the party."

Cararro looked perplexed. A five year old wouldn't be much of a catch.

He sat back in his chair and nodded. "I guess that it wouldn't have had much influence on you then. But tell me when you learned about your mother."

"My father had a heart attack in 1965 and, when I visited him in the hospital, he wanted to talk about my mother. She'd died in 1961. He told me that she'd carried a card. He died just a few days later."

Agent Cararro eyes flashed and a triumphant smile broke out. "Are you telling me your father made a deathbed confession?"

I was furious but said simply, "I didn't consider it a confession. My father didn't give a shit about Communism; he'd just wanted me to know about my mother."

"Mr. Meades, this is new information. Is there anything else you think we need to know? What will we discover in the Extended Background Investigation? You went to Wisconsin. Who were your professors? Were they lefties? How about taking that polygraph?"

My secret was exposed. I didn't see any downside to the polygraph. "I'll have to ask my lawyer but I think it's likely he'll agree. May I call you to schedule a test?"

Agent Cararro left and I thought that was the end of it. My nasty little secret was out, so the poly would be a breeze. It was irrelevant, I mused, but if a five year old couldn't get a clearance, no one could. Still, to be safe, I called my lawyer, Don Feldman. He suggested that before I schedule a poly with DIS I take a private examination, for practice.

"You never know," he said, "Once you're in there they could ask anything. Let's see how you do under pressure—before we place your balls on the block."

"All right," I said. "Schedule one."

"Hey, my Uncle Harry was a Red. Are you sure there isn't anything you need to tell me now?"

I stifled the urge to tell him, "Fuck You."

●●●

The practice polygraph was scheduled for a week later. When I presented myself in Feldman's office he introduced me to the examiner and left the room. The examiner hooked me up to the machine.

"Okay, Mr. Meades. I'm going to connect several monitoring devices—a finger sensor to measure perspiration, a cuff to monitor your blood pressure, and a halter around your chest that measures your breathing patterns. Experience tells us that these are the most likely variables that change when a person is being deceptive."

I didn't feel comfortable but I went along with the routine, eager to learn as much as possible about the methodology. He explained the procedure.

"First," he said, "we'll discuss the questions to ensure that you understand them. Each answer must be a simple yes or no, and any ambiguity or uncertainty in the questions must be resolved, before we begin the examination."

"What?" I said. "You mean I can't explain an answer?"

"No, we go through all of that before the test. The questions I pose will reflect our discussion."

I wasn't happy but I nodded. Then, he described how he would ask some simple questions to calibrate me—I had to be truthful on some of these questions, and deliberately lie on others, such as "Is Meades your name? Were you born on such and such?"

We began.

"So Mr. Meades, is that your name?"

"Yes," I replied and watched the needles stay more or less constant as they drew straight lines on the recording paper.

"Are you married?"

"No," I lied as instructed and watched the needles jump, leaving zigzag lines on the recording paper.

We then went into the test in earnest.

Twenty minutes later the examiner said, "Mr. Meades, I have to tell you that your answers are coming across as deceptive. Since we're not testing for anything in reality, you must have a guilty personality. You will fail any test unless you learn how to relax."

I smiled grimly and he removed the monitoring sensors. After I wrote the man a check for two hundred dollars he left and Feldman returned to the room.

"The examiner told me that you probably should not take the DIS test." Feldman was smiling and I didn't like it. He enjoyed gallows humor and it was coming through, loud and clear.

"I have to take the test," I said, "but now I regret the practice session. How the hell am I going to relax? I've been guilty my whole life. For Christ's sake, I'm a Jew."

● ● ●

The month before the test was horrible. My job was on the line and I couldn't get the test out of my mind. I noticed more and more articles about Communists in the newspapers. The Soviets landed a probe on the moon and it was as though the Red Menace were back.

To prepare myself, I took no medications and avoided booze the previous night. In the morning I ran six miles around the hills behind Stanford. I chanted Buddhist mantras. I practiced biofeedback techniques in the car, hoping to contain my nervousness.

The exam was in the Federal Building on Golden Gate Avenue in San Francisco. DIS is on the tenth floor and the elevator stopped at every floor. On the way up I saturated my shirt with sweat and considered giving up and returning home. Then I reasoned that there might not be any sweat left.

Agent Cararro greeted me in the office along with Investigator Ryan, who would administer the test. They were rather distant but professional. After a few moments it was just me and the investigator in the room—but there was a one-way mirror and I knew Cararro was on the other side.

"Mr. Meades," Investigator Ryan said, "have you ever taken a polygraph examination before?"

"No, er . . . yes, I have."

"I see. And that was under what circumstances?"

"Well, I took a practice test last month in my lawyer's office, you know, to see what it's all about?"

I thought Ryan was distracted by his machine, which was warming up with needles moving all over the paper. But he was alert. "You took a practice session? To learn how to beat the machine? Is that it, Mr. Meades? Do you have something to hide?"

At that point it seemed like everything I'd done to get top secret clearance were futile. The careful answers, the hedging, the practice poly—it had all turned into evidence of guilt. I looked at Ryan sheepishly. "No, it was nothing like that. I was just nervous."

"All right, Mr. Meades. We'll see. Apparently, you know the routine. Here are the questions I'm going to ask."

We went through his questions. Was Meades my name? Was I born in Evanston, Illinois in 1938? Did I smoke marijuana? Had I gone to Roosevelt High School? Did I graduate from the University of Wisconsin? Had I ever knowingly disclosed classified information to a person not cleared for that information? Did I have relatives behind the Iron Curtain? On and on it went but not one of the questions focused on my mother.

I watched the machine during the test and except for the test questions in which I was directed to lie, not once did the needles jump. I had just begun to relax when Investigator Ryan said, "Thank you, Mr. Meades. Those are all the questions. *Now, is there anything else you want to tell me?*"

Alarm bells went off in my head. The needles exploded, bouncing all over the paper. Twenty-eight years of guilt poured out of my mind. Stealing a nickel from my grandmother's purse; throwing stones at cars; accidentally hitting a girl in the head with a golf club; cheating on a high school Spanish test; buying a hot TV. My mother never entered my thoughts. Crestfallen I looked at Ryan.

The investigator smiled. "Relax, Mr. Meades. That question doesn't count. We're just having fun. We do that to everybody. Remember? We have to review the questions first."

● ● ●

The letter went directly to MDRI. The director of security informed me I had received my clearance and briefed me on the procedures for handling top secret documents. I was elated and went to the project office to access the classified reports. The project administrator took me into a secure facility and gave me the combination to a classified document container.

I must have looked at hundreds of pages that day. Every one of them described the behavior of space interceptors and ICBMs. They were filled with equations that I recognized. I wondered if it had been worth the gauntlet of stress to see Newton's classical equations of motion; they'd been derived three hundred years ago and were in any freshman's physics text. The equations were stamped TOP SECRET.

Ben and Greta

Late one afternoon in February, Greta von Hohenzollern-Becker sat at the bar of the Aspen Lodge looking out the window at an advanced double black diamond ski run. A fire roared in the corner fireplace and the strong aroma of burning wood flavored the air. Greta, like many wealthy women who'd been raised in Europe, was well dressed. She was in her sixties but still had a fashion runway figure. She wore tight, form fitting beige ski pants, black après-ski boots, and a red cashmere sweater, capped by an expensive Hermès scarf which sported a hunt scene in India.

Greta was on her second double, extra-dry, Absolut vodka martini, ruminating on the lack of excitement in her life, when some lunatic on the ski run captured her attention. He was going about forty miles per hour without poles. She watched as he caught an edge, crossed his skis, and took a monumental fall. A few moments later the Ski Patrol pulled him out of the snow and brought him down to the foot of the mountain, where he shrugged off any assistance and stumbled into the lodge. Given the seriousness of the fall Greta thought the man must be in excellent condition—and a little crazy, too.

A few minutes later the fool was sitting next to her at the bar. He was covered with snow which melted and dripped, forming a pool of water on the floor below his stool. He seemed oblivious to the snow still trapped in his hair and jammed down his collar.

"That's quite a fall you took."

"Good thing I was stoned, or I might have been hurt." He smiled playfully, grabbed a few bar napkins to blow his nose, and waved for the bartender.

"Well, I'm trying to get stoned myself," said Greta. "My husband's in Bermuda playing golf and I'm bored silly."

My goodness, she wondered. *Did I really say that?* She looked at him; he was shorter than her and a little older. He looked kind of cute.

"What's your name?" he asked.

"Greta. Greta von Hohenzollern-Becker."

"Where are you from? That name, it sounds German."

"I was born in Rasternburg, originally a Prussian town. But I live in San Francisco now."

"Greta, I'm Ben," he said. "Ben Schneider, from Chicago. Do you know how to play Nim?"

"I don't believe so."

Ben described the game of Nim, in which several rows of increasing numbers of coins, from two to five, were aligned, and then players removed any number of coins, from any single row, on each move.

"The last one to remove a coin," he said, "is the loser. I never lose."

"How can that be? What if I go first?"

"Greta, let's play. You can go first, or second. If you lose, I'll buy you a drink."

"What if I win?"

Ben grinned. "How about I buy you a drink?"

They called the bartender over and asked for a stack of quarters.

●●●

The next morning was a blur. Greta's head pounded. The bed was a mess and her clothes were piled on a chair. A half-full martini glass was on the dresser and an empty beer bottle lay on the floor. Greta vaguely remembered drinking more martinis and falling off her stool. She had a picture in her mind of Ben helping her to her room. She rolled over in the bed and was startled to see Ben coming out of the bathroom. He was dressed and he had a big grin.

"Greta," he said, "You were wonderful. You're very exciting. Thank you for this special gift."

"Oh my God! What am I going to tell my husband? I've never done anything like this before."

"Greta, don't worry about it. You think he's playing golf twenty-four hours a day? I got to go or we'd do it again. Take care."

After Ben left, Greta lay in bed and stretched languidly. She smiled and thought about the evening. She'd had sex for the first time in fifteen years. She wasn't sure but she thought she had complained about her husband. He deserved it, she decided—a little revenge. *It was about time the Goose got even with the Gander.* Despite her hangover she felt strangely fulfilled. She wished Ben had stayed. He was exciting. Greta eyed the unfinished martini.

●●●

Ben flew back to Chicago. That evening he met his buddies for their monthly poker game in Sandburg Village, near the Gold Coast of Chicago.

"I had an unbelievable tumble," Ben said with a laugh. "I broke a ski and my binding on a double black diamond run. Damn near broke my neck. The Ski Patrol had to bring me down the mountain. Then I met this drunken woman—sort of attractive, too—in the bar. Her name was Greta von Hohen-something and she reminded me of Greta von Nostrand from cable TV. You guys know I can't stand TV commentators so I bought her another drink, you know, for fun; to see if I could liquor her up."

Alan, Ben's racquetball partner who sold life insurance, was listening with a mischievous look and said, "So? I thought you can't get it up since you had your prostate removed."

"I can't," said Ben with a smile, "and neither can you, asshole. You ain't got one either. But we got drunk as skunks. She was a real talker. Her husband was in Bermuda and it sounded to me like he was with his latest squeeze. I think she was looking for a little payback. But I liked her."

"So what happened?" asked Barry, the best poker player in the bunch who was counting his chips.

"I introduced her to the game of Nim. We played for drinks. About an hour later she fell off her stool. I helped her to her room and ended up spending the night. The next morning I faked it, told her she'd been a great lay for an old babe, and left her smiling."

Barry was curious. "She actually thought you guys had screwed?"

"I guess so," said Ben, "she was really loaded."

"Did you get her phone number?" asked Alan with a grin.

"Why, you want to sell her husband some insurance?"

"I figure if we can get her between us, we could, maybe, each get by with a half a hard-on."

The men roared but Ben frowned. He'd been thinking about Greta and wondered how she was doing. He fingered a note with her phone number and reached for his phone.

●●●

Greta returned to San Francisco and called her husband in Bermuda. She told him the marriage was over—he could move in with that bimbo he was screwing down there. California was a community property state and she was keeping the apartment in Pacific Heights, the Merrill Lynch Cash Management Account, the vineyards in Napa, and the Mercedes. He could have everything else.

"But what happened?" asked her husband.

"Sex happened, you ninny. I realized what I've been missing. But no, not you, you've been chasing every skirt in town. What? Did you think I didn't know? I have a lover now and I'm going to have some fun. You can tell the children. Good-bye."

The phone rang and she smiled when Caller ID indicated the call was from an area code in Chicago.

"Greta? It's Ben. How're you doing?"

"I'm so glad you called. I'd like to see you again."

"Greta, I have a confession. I like you but I have to tell you that we really didn't make love. I can't do it; I've had surgery and it doesn't work anymore."

"Ben," she said, "I don't care. Bring the quarters. I've got the Absolut. I've dumped my husband. When can we meet?"

"But Greta, there was no sex. Do you understand that?"

"Ben, I need excitement and you're an exciting man. I can pretend too."

The Greatest Roman—Ever

After Gaius Julius Caesar was assassinated in bc 44, a second civil war loomed. Historians documented the murder and the war—even Shakespeare wrote of both. Consider the question: What if some of the major players, in particular, Marcus Tullius Cicero and Gaius Julius Caesar, had character flaws unknown to history, What if they had certain deficiencies in their personalities? Would things have been different? Perhaps not. The Great Comet of bc 44, recorded also by the Chinese, was en route to Earth.

● ● ●

Gaius Julius Caesar, the most powerful man in the world, was unhappy. Women swooned at his feet; his legions loved him, even when he decimated troops whose loyalty proved lacking. He mocked and humbled his political enemies by sleeping with their wives. But Caesar, defeater of Vercingetorix and his army of 330,000 Gauls, was lonely. His closest friend, Marcus Crassus, the richest man in Rome, had been killed in battle. Caesar's mother, Aurelia, the classiest and brightest woman in Rome, was dead. Daughter Julia, the light of his life, married for political advantage to that ass, Gnaeus Pompeius Magnus, the self-named Great Pompey—dead too; in childbirth, along with the grandson that Caesar had longed for.

Caesar had a wife, of course, beyond reproach. But, in the political arena, in the contest for power, she mattered little. Calpurnia was sweet, and faithful, but she lacked the intellect to challenge or excite Caesar.

No, Caesar, a war hero and senator at twenty, a senior consul of Rome and dictator by acclamation, the greatest general since Sulla and Marius, a descendant of Venus, was alone and, worse, he felt inadequate. He craved, no; he could not live without, the approval of Marcus Tullius Cicero. And therein lay the rub. Cicero detested Caesar's ambition, worshiped the Republic, and was convinced Caesar schemed to be King of Rome.

Caesar couldn't explain his childish obsession for Cicero's respect. Perhaps, he thought, it was because Cicero was a greater orator. There were the usual fawning fools in the Senate, of course, who pandered to Caesar. And, the citizens revered him. But, deep down, Caesar knew better—Cicero was a smarter man, more eloquent, and a greater advocate.

If only Cicero could bend to Caesar's *dignitas*. They could rule the world together!

Further, Caesar was frustrated. He lacked a Roman heir. He had children scattered here and there; a few in Gaul and he'd even fathered Brutus' younger sister, but the customs of Rome dictated that he could not acknowledge any of the children; nor did he want to. Of his two closest male relatives, his cousin, Marcus Antonius was the politically correct choice, but Antonius was a drunk, sadistic, profligate spender, always in debt, a womanizing barbarian, and hated by his legions. The alternative was Caesar's grand nephew, Octavian, but the boy was young, effeminate, and always wheezing with asthma. Still, Octavian seemed to be bright and Caesar had no choice but to secretly name the lad in his will.

Adding to his problems, Caesar's enemies in the Senate, led by Cato and Cassius, plied him with professed honors he didn't want; which embarrassed him, and fueled further jealousy and hatred among the other senators. Statues were erected to Caesar which inferred that he was already a god. They reinforced the illusion the dictator craved greater power. Caesar couldn't believe anyone really thought he wanted to be a god or King. He released his lictors, his personal bodyguards, to demonstrate that he didn't require special protection. That proved fatal when twenty-three of his senatorial colleagues murdered him on the floor of the Senate, in the most famous assassination in antiquity.

●●●

"'Caesar was an ambitious man,' said Brutus—married to that lunatic Porcia, daughter of Cato. He was encouraged to kill Caesar, dictator of Rome and my cousin, by both his wife and his mother, Servilia. That bitch was spurned by Caesar and we all know scorned women are dangerous!"

"My name is Marcus Antonius and I'm in the prime of my life. I rule Rome with two other consuls—Octavius, Octavian, whatever they call him—that fairy, he even calls himself Caesar now—and Marcus Lepidus, my puppet. We call it a Triumvirate but I'm senior. Women melt in my presence. I command armies and win battles. So what if my men hate me? None of that sentimental just-one-of-the-boys crap that Caesar spewed—although I must admit his men idolized him. Oh, he always said it was just his *dignitas* that mattered; that he didn't want to be King or be treated like a god. What nonsense! No one believed such denials. We all want to be a god; we all want to be King. And why didn't he make me his heir instead of that pansy great nephew of his? He even adopted him, made Octavius his son. Why not me? I was his Master of the Horse, the ruler of Rome in his absence. It was all because of that damn Cicero who complicated things and confounded Caesar.

"I knew about the plot, of course, and did nothing to stop it. Why would I? It was obvious that I was the heir to that enormous wealth; it would have left me an inexhaustible supply of money, even after satisfying my horrendous debts. Caesar was rich beyond belief and it all would have been mine! But, I couldn't risk getting involved either way; if the plot failed it would have been the end of me, if it succeeded I was set for life. I never dreamed I wouldn't be the heir. That stupid will; leaving everything to that skinny faggot, Octavian.

"Why did the dictator ever give up his lictors? If he were still alive I would continue to bask in the glory of second-in-command, and, more importantly, be heir-apparent. Didn't he understand human nature? Power is everything! It means money, women, the finest wine, and more women.

"It would have been so simple if Cicero had cooperated with the dictator. Instead, in the orator's absence, Caesar grew sullen and withdrawn, the Senate became unmanageable, and chaos reigned in the courts. Unrest grew and the plot expanded. The assassins never would have recruited Brutus, a patrician absolutely necessary to legitimatize their act, if the conditions in the Senate had been different.

"But would Cicero deign to give Rome a respite, some peace? Would he cooperate with Caesar? Would he come to a Senate meeting? No, the windbag said he wouldn't participate in Caesar's dictatorship; that to do so would be to make him complicit in the death of the Republic. He could have easily stopped the plot if he knew about it. But no, he had to shun the meetings of the Senate—where he undoubtedly would have learned about the conspiracy. And then afterwards, the coward reveled in Caesar's death and supported the tyrannicide. I was forced to give the killers a free pass. If Cicero had only prosecuted them, they'd all be dead now, and no one could ever learn that I knew of the plot.

"Well, Cicero has gone too far, attacking me in the Senate. Great speeches perhaps; the man's a wonderful speaker. But how dare he accuse me of treason, to suggest that I'm a greater threat to the Republic than Caesar, to call me a deadbeat? That's too much. What is it with this stupid longing for a Republic, anyway? Why didn't Caesar just kill him? What nerve has Cicero; to say that I was the *real* murderer of Caesar? This time I'm going to get him! Jupiter damn Cicero!"

●●●

Cicero accumulated villas with gifts from his legal clients the way other men collected war trophies, sexual conquests, and fine art. He had properties scattered across Italy. Retreating from Rome to one of his homes, after his latest senatorial diatribe against Antonius, Cicero was worried. It was not just his attack on Antonius. How long, he wondered, could he maintain his façade? They all thought he was a genius and a pillar of justice—yet Cicero knew it was a lie. It had been luck and craven manipulation, he thought, and opportunity after opportunity to exploit people dumber than him. It was not that he thought he was bright; he sensed he wasn't. It was just that most people were stupid. He marveled how he'd been in the right place at the right time. That glib tongue had even got him elected Senior Consul once.

Cicero knew he couldn't manage his way out of a litter without a slave's assistance. He couldn't even find his way around the Forum without following someone. He was astonished that Caesar had pardoned him during the earlier civil war; after all, he spoke continuously against Caesar and supported fools like Cato, Cassius, and the rest of those murderous idiots. Why, he asked himself, did the dictator cloy at him, solicit his advice, his friendship, and his collaboration in the Senate? Cicero knew he wasn't up to the task—Caesar would have seen right through him had they worked together. And now, he'd stuck his foot in his mouth once more, attacking Antonius in speech after speech in the Senate. Thank Jupiter, Cicero thought; he was a senator, protected by Roman law. Otherwise his head would be on the block or, worse, they'd throw him off the Tarpeian Rock.

●●●

Gaius Octavius Julius Caesar coughed as usual. It was his bloody asthma. Stress didn't help, and there was no lack of that now. Sharing power with Antonius and Lepidus was complicated and dangerous. Lepidus constituted a nothing, he thought, who could be disposed of at will. But Antonius was a different matter. He plotted to grab total power—a serious threat to young Octavius. Fortunately, Octavius knew that Antonius believed he could manipulate him, and that he lacked political acumen. Antonius had ignored the fact, reflected Octavius, that he'd spent months at the foot of the dictator—the smartest man in the world—drinking in every word. And Caesar had respected him; that's why he'd adopted him, made him son of Caesar, and heir to everything. Octavius could call himself Caesar. Of course, absconding with Caesar's war chest immediately after the assassination had helped him bribe the troops—and positioned him to be elected the youngest consul in history—even Cicero voted for him. Octavius might not have Antonius' physique, military reputation, or his way with women; but he had the money, brains, and the positioning to grab power.

Still, there was a Triumvirate, a shaky structure, forged in haste to avoid another civil war. So Octavius thought it necessary to bide his time. To continue to let Antonius and the Senate think he was just an ineffective child, who lusted only to avenge his father's death. Fortunately Antonius was furious at Cicero. Octavius figured he'd let Antonius kill Cicero. He could move to consolidate power afterwards. He asked himself why interfere? Cicero was pro-Republic and could be a problem, even with his weaknesses. The man was a pompous fool. Why, he wondered, did his father ever pander to Cicero? Why did people, even smart people, act like sycophants in the presence of people that were so-called intellectuals? Sure, Cicero could talk, and even write. But the new Caesar had noticed that Cicero was bewildered most of the time. Cicero didn't fool him. Under that visage there lurked an idiot. Just as soon as Cicero was dead, Octavius thought, he would eliminate Antonius—who most certainly had known of the assassination plot, had enabled it by his inaction, and had failed in his responsibilities to protect the dictator. Revenge, and power—those were the reasons Antonius had to die. Meanwhile the Triumvirate would proscribe, and thereby fatten the purse of Rome with the confiscated wealth of outlawed senators.

When the time came, he knew that it would be simple to exploit the omen, the great comet which had thundered through the sky the day of the dictator's funeral. The comet, a gift from Jupiter, was a signal to all of Rome that Caesar was a god. As Caesar's heir, that made Gaius Octavius Julius Caesar a god too! He would add Augustus to his name and become Emperor of Rome. He, a short, wasted, boyish weakling, unskilled with women, and a political neophyte, would master Rome, the greatest empire in the world. One that had endured for five hundred years!

●●●

Centurions ordered by Antonius to kill Cicero and to bring back his head and hands—those "damn hands that have written so much drivel"—found Cicero, in a litter on the Via Appia, escorted by a small entourage of slaves. Cicero, panicky, and with less awareness than usual, managed to get his head out of the litter just before it was lopped off. The centurions dragged his body out, cut off his hands, and left the rest of Cicero lying on the road. They nailed his head and hands to the gates of Rome and the Senate mourned the loss of its brightest light.

Without the moderating influence of Cicero, Rome exploded in a new civil war between Antonius and the new Caesar. Outgeneraled, outwitted, and outspent by the "little twerp," Antonius retreated into the eastern provinces, to a conquest of Cleopatra, and to defeat in battle at the hand of Octavius' troops.

In the end, young Gaius Octavius Julius Caesar Augustus defeated all of his enemies, manipulated the entire political establishment of Rome, and became the first Emperor and god of Rome. Augustus ruled for forty-one years in one of the longest and most peaceful reigns in Roman history. He established a political dynasty that ruled for generations. As the greatest Emperor, he competed only with his father, Gaius Julius Caesar and Marcus Tullius Cicero, whom history lionized for his intellect, for the title of the greatest Roman—ever.

Day of Infamy

Kochira wa Nagano-san desu . . . Excuse me. Hello, my name is Satoru Nagano. I forgot I was writing to an English audience. My American friends asked me to tell you what happened on that day in Japan, a very long time ago.

It was late that night. There were rumors of war spreading throughout the country. I'd heard some people say it was a sneak attack. Others thought it was inevitable; that they'd been forced into it by the global competition for resources. Professor Goto, from *Todai* University (University of Tokyo), interviewed on NHK radio, was dismayed. He pronounced, "It was due to the world's Robinson Crusoe economy, in which one must trade-off desires and wants with limited available resources."

American radio said that it was provoked by the typical human craving for power. Other media were hysterical. European stations talked about world domination. Brussels scoffed. Germany was not upset; of course, it already had deals with Japan. But otherwise, in most capitals, resolve was called for. Most people were somber, anticipating hardships and casualties.

In the Fujitsu factory in Numazu we were very concerned. It was a different day, in Japan, than in America, when it happened. If I recall, it was late on a Monday, when we actually heard about it. Numazu is in Shizuoka Prefecture, between Tokyo and Nagoya. We'd assembled for dinner—it was after I'd watched the sun set over Suruga Bay. A football game had ended when they alerted us to a National Pronouncement so all shifts assembled in the dining room. The room seethed with excitement, fear, and greed. They said that we would have to expand the assembly lines and that we would be manufacturing more equipment. It was war and we were going to become profiteers!

I could understand how many people in the west probably felt confused and threatened. This was a watershed moment; things were going to change. On one hand, it was a very exciting time; Janis Joplin was entertaining enthusiastic crowds in America; and a new Chief Justice of the United States Supreme Court was sworn into office. But not everything was positive; that day the Cuyahoga River caught fire, there were intense floods in Tennessee as ten inches of rain fell in five hours on the Salt Lick Creek watershed; in Italy the Vatican removed forty saints from its liturgical calendar; and in France the government of Couve de Murville resigned. Globally, the omens were not auspicious. This conflict was going to leave old industries and nations; those that couldn't adapt, in smoking ruins. People were going to lose more than their jobs.

In Japan, no one knew how it would turn out. This was breaking new ground. It was going to establish a new order of things, a new co-prosperity sphere. But there was doubt, too. Economists were divided. How would the people react? Would they understand? How would the markets react? Would the history books tell the truth?

The people looked to the throne for guidance. The Emperor summoned the Foreign Minister and the Minister of Industry and Trade to his chambers. After twelve hours of intense discussions, the Emperor issued a proclamation, "To Our good and loyal subjects: We crave only peace and justice for the peoples of the world. We shall weather this storm together, and through strength, determination, a common sharing of the burden, and faith in *Shichi-Fuku-Jin*, the seven gods of good fortune, We shall prevail." Even our factory was honored by an enthusiastic and encouraging letter from the Chrysanthemum Throne.

Yes, things were complicated around the world, that day, June 23, 1969, a day that will live in infamy—the day that IBM unbundled, separately priced its applications software from its hardware, and the day the Software Industry was born. It also was the day the Software Wars began. Software was no longer free.

/S/

Nagano Satoru
Fujitsu Systems Engineer, Retired
Yokohama, Japan

Cesspool Charlie

Cesspool was not the nickname given Charlie by his parents. It was laid down on him by a bunch of horny-handed miners—in a moment of doubtful judgment on the part of Charlie.

Charlie was a hard-rock silver miner noted for his expertise with dynamite. And folks in Panamint Valley had a high regard for Charlie's skills; it was said that he could shape his charges with such precision that he'd blast a pocket of ore a mere fifteen feet from his corn liquor and lunch—knowing full well that his stash was safe. Sober, his confidence was not misplaced and his accuracy was unmatched. Three-Fingers McGraw always said that he could outperform Charlie, but the other miners knew that Three-Fingers would never risk a precious bottle of booze.

Things came to a head when Jack Baggin, proprietor of the Last Chance Mine built a house. He had a new bride, Annie Rose McGonagle who had worked at the Trona Saloon. Annie had dated several of the miners in her day including Charlie, searching for the right man. Jack, with a fortune in silver, based to a considerable extent on the skills of Charlie, seemed to be the right man. Jack built the house on some High Sierra granite, in a nice part of town. He stuffed it with new furniture and affixed the latest in lightning rods. With the house complete from A to Z, Jack and Annie announced a house-warming party and invited miners from Inyo and San Bernardino counties—all the way from Lone Pine in the north, down through Trona, and west to Lake Isabella. The miners and their women assembled and the liquor began to flow.

Now this may seem improbable but it was discovered, shortly after the party commenced, that someone had erred—there was no cesspool. And the house wasn't sitting on nice, soft, easy-digging Illinois loam. Annie, of course, was out of sorts. One would expect a house to have a cesspool. Jack proposed a new outhouse to Annie but she stormed away. The marriage was too young for her to nag, but Jack knew that the outhouse idea was a dog that wouldn't hunt. He called Charlie over and gave him the assignment. As special compensation he offered Charlie a bottle of bourbon with a real label on the bottle.

Perhaps Jack's reason to gift a bottle of the devil's brew to Charlie was to ease his toil, or to wet his whistle, or it was just an act of generosity. Those who were there that day weren't sure—but they all agreed that it was a lapse of judgment on Jack's part.

No one knows how it happened; whether Charlie was seized by a mischievous imp, a jealous devil, if it was an accident, or caused by the brew itself—although it was common knowledge that Charlie could chug a quart of rye and walk a straight line. In any event, Charlie knocked off the bottle and went to work. He sized up the job, ran his hands over the granite, tapped here and there, put his ear to the stone, and drilled a few holes. He planted his charges, lit the fuses, and BAM! Besides the rather oversized hole for the cesspool that appeared after the dust settled, the explosion shattered all the windows in the new house and blew out half the windows in the neighborhood. It lifted the roof a full six inches off the rafters, and let fly an enormous boulder that smashed the keg of bourbon that Jack had ordered for the party. The explosion was ringing in everyone's ears when the roof slammed down and shattered tiles went airborne, showering the partygoers. Charlie had the good sense to take to the hills. Out of whiskey, the party wound down.

●●●

Several years later, a hiker ran into Charlie up in the hills beyond Beatty. Charlie was camped with his two burros, bearing prospecting gear, tied off to a bush, and brewing a pot of coffee.

"Name's Charlie, sit yourself down and have a cup."

"Wow. You wouldn't be Cesspool Charlie by any chance—would you?" asked the hiker. "You're supposed to be one of the blanket Jackass prospectors in these parts. They tell stories about you in the Trona Saloon."

Charlie poured some red whisky into both cups of coffees.

"Yup, that's me."

"What happened that day at Jack Baggin's? How could you make a mistake like that with all your demolitions experience?"

"Weren't no mistake!"

"Were you drunk?"

"I was sober as a durn Mormon."

"Then I don't understand," said the hiker. "From what I heard, the cesspool was three times bigger than it had to be."

"Jack Baggin is full of shit and I figgered he needed a big one," replied Charlie as he stared into his cup.

"Do you think you deserve that name Cesspool?"

"Sure I deserve it," he said with candor. "It was too bad about that keg of whiskey but, you see Annie and me, we was sweet on each other. She was working in the Trona Saloon and Baggin stole her off me by bribing her with that new house. He paid for it with my sweat, too—it was me that found the silver vein in the Last Chance Mine. That explosion weren't no mistake, but for the fact the boulder missed Baggin. It was damn close too, just a foot off."

Charlie smiled wistfully and poured some more red whisky into his cup.

"Let me tell ya," he continued, "what with Annie, her momma and six kids, that cesspool is filling up. Baggin, that cheap bastard, like as not ain't never had it pumped out. Someday I'm gonna sneak up there after dark with some dynamite and a long fuse. That redneck's never gonna forget Cesspool Charlie.

The Test

Chester P. Hurley, the loan officer and manager at the branch of Chase Manhattan Bank, located on the northwest corner of Madison Avenue and 69th Street, shrugged nonchalantly.

"Another check to jamaicaprocessing.com? How much this time?"

His assistant, Kathryn, studied the check. "It's $68,000 this time—the amounts have been slowly increasing over the last few months."

Hurley nodded. "Well, it's no big deal. Spinoza's a high-end client and it's all covered by his line of credit—and that's guaranteed by his home. Why do you keep bringing the checks to me?"

"I'm just trying to follow the rules; all overdrafts require your approval."

"Okay." Chester initialed the check and smiled appraisingly at Kathryn. She was twenty-two, a recent graduate of Hunter College, with legs that went to the moon. Boy, he thought, if he only had Spinoza's money, he'd bag her in no time.

"All the previous checks have been covered," he said, "I'm sure this one is no different."

As Kathryn left his corner office, which was nestled up to the window on Madison, Hurley reflected on his meeting with Spinoza.

"That's right, Mr. Spinoza. We can let you have a line of credit on your Westchester home—right now the bank can go $7 Million on your home equity of $9.5 Million. I might get more, too—if you're willing to disclose your tax returns."

Alex Spinoza, a heavy set man with a dark complexion, thinning hair, and freckled hands smiled. "That's nice, Hurley. But I don't really need the money now. I just want to establish a slush fund, you know, for cash flow in case some options present themselves."

"I know, you said that in the application. But don't worry; we don't start charging until you actually draw down the line and the rate is one point below prime."

Hurley had wondered if Spinoza really didn't need the money, but the officers had approved the line so who was he to second guess the loan? Still, he'd thought Spinoza had a sleazy look. But that was the banking business—you had to deal with all kind of assholes. Turning in his chair, Hurley looked out the window. He was rewarded with the sight of Kathryn hurrying down Madison Avenue. The wind pressed her dress against those magnificent legs, highlighting them. All thoughts of Spinoza disappeared.

●●●

At the same time the wind gave Hurley a treat, computers in a huge datacenter in Norman, Oklahoma—a centralized credit card bureau—processed three $35,000 charges to Visa, MasterCard and Discover Card accounts. All the charges were from a company identified as jamaicaprocessing.com, headquartered on the Isle of Man in the English Channel. The company ran Internet servers and was a blind cut-out established by PokerPlayerOnLine.com, a Hong Kong gambling site, to circumvent U.S. laws against on-line gambling.

The machines in Norman, Oklahoma had been programmed to detect extraordinary, or fraudulent, charges. But their artificial intelligence routines, supported by neural network software which "learned" how to filter good transactions from bad, had been lulled into a false sense of complacency. Many similar transactions in the past all had proved authentic. The charges were approved by the computers and jamaicaprocessing.com moved the funds immediately to a player account on PokerPlayerOnLine.com—where they were converted to Hong Kong dollars. Several days later, PokerPlayerOnLine. com was instructed, by the player, to relay by wire the funds, in Euros, to an account at Deutsche Bank, in Frankfurt.

●●●

Two months later, Alex Spinoza slammed the accelerator to the floor. The view of the trees in the forests along the side of German Autobahn 8 blurred as his speed increased to two hundred, then two hundred twenty kilometers per hour. Exits for Augsburg flew by, and then Ulm, as he raced toward Karlsruhe and the road to Baden-Baden. Spinoza mentally computed the speed in miles per hour of his brand new black BMW M5—one hundred thirty-two. His math was good—it had to be for a fledgling embezzler and identity thief.

Spinoza, fifty-nine, was a successful accountant, owning a small CPA firm in southern Manhattan. To reduce his commute to Westchester, he'd purchased a small apartment in Battery Park City—it was also an excuse not to go home. He'd been married thirty years and couldn't stand his wife. More than once he'd considered leaving but he was repelled by the thought of giving up half his wealth—New York was a community-property state. That was before he'd come up with a scheme for stealing substantially more than half of what he would have owed his wife; enough money so that the unthinkable, divorce, had become thinkable. In fact, the desire to dump his wife had become a flame raging in his gut.

Alex had studied identity theft methods for months before he'd put his plan to this test. It was great, he thought, the perfect victimless crime. The only ones that would get screwed were the banks and the credit card companies. Funny, he thought, if his wife only knew the trouble he was going to—which might give her *all* the family money—she'd love him even more for it—as if it mattered. Well, unless they came after her for the money. But Alex didn't give a damn about that, and, he'd be free!

He'd researched conventional schemes for hustling identities, e.g., counterfeiting checks, rifling mailboxes for credit card applications, and stealing credit card numbers from restaurant and bar charge slips. He'd discovered that social security numbers were a-dime-a-dozen on the Internet, along with birth and marriage data, death certificates, residential histories, and credit reports. Spinoza had also learned how to launder funds through on-line poker websites. The M5, fetched just yesterday from BMW headquarters, near the *Olympia Zentrum*, in Munich, and a remaining bank balance in Germany of almost $72,000 were proof his system worked. Oh, he'd have to pay for the car—that would generate a load of bullshit from his wife too, of course—and give the rest of the money back, but the test worked and the pump was primed. After this experiment he was going for the jugular—the entire $7 Million in the line of credit.

He smiled as he looked over at his passenger. Jutta Becker's red hair fluttered in the wind that whipped through the car from the open sun-roof. She didn't seem to mind; her eyes were glazed with excitement as the M5 approached two hundred fifty kilometers per hour. Gorgeous, thought Spinoza—and smart. Jutta, 36, was a German national he'd met on the flight to Munich; she spoke five languages and was a graduate of the University of Heidelberg. She'd grown up in the *Schwarzwald*, the Black Forest, and she'd promised to give Alex a tour after they'd spent the weekend at the Brenner Park Hotel in Baden-Baden. It made for a promising adventure, he thought—except for that rotten little dog she had in her lap. It was furless and stared back at him with large black eyes filled with hate.

"How's the dog doing?" He asked over the howl of the wind.

"Sigmund? He's fine but we're going too fast to let him stick his head out of the window."

Too bad, thought Alex. Maybe the wind would suck Sigmund right out of the car. "Isn't there something we can do about him? He's always climbing onto my back when we make love."

"Don't be silly, Sigmund just wants to be loved too."

Spinoza felt like throwing the dog out the sun-roof. That would make for an interesting sight in his rear view mirror, he mused, but he nodded and kept his silence—better to not be distracted at these speeds. Although the autobahns had long stretches of road with unrestricted speeds, there were periodic speed limits and construction zones that demanded a driver's attention.

When Spinoza turned south onto Autobahn 5, he reflected on his grand plan. Stealing identities was nothing, he thought—the twist was to steal your own identity—that was class! He was going to steal from himself and give the money back to himself! He'd created a duplicate Alex Spinoza, based on the death of a young man named Alejandro Spinoza in Springfield, Illinois in 1950.

The plan was brilliant: Construct a duplicate identity with another real social security number, both mined on-line from death certificates; establish an address through a mail drop in Europe, get an overseas bank account for the new identity, and build a pattern of charges on his existing credit cards, in shady establishments where credit card knock-offs were not uncommon. He'd also moved large amounts of funds through on-line poker sites that used credit card servers that masked their real identities. He didn't even have to gamble, just deposit and then move the money.

As Alex slowed to drive through an *Umleitung* (detour), he recalled his meeting at Deutsche Bank in Frankfurt.

"So, Herr Spinoza, you wish to open a Eurocheque and Eurocard account?" the bank officer had asked. He'd been a *Graf*, a member of one of the landed family aristocracies in Germany.

"I need the account so I can write checks in Euros, Pounds, or Danish Crowns, and a Eurocard to draw upon the funds at ATM machines."

"And the amount of the initial deposit?"

"One thousand in cash, American dollars. I expect to make several large deposits by wire over the next year."

Spinoza, at the time, had not known the amounts he would deposit. But he knew there would be only two transactions; the results of one actual test, with real money, and then the grand finale. He'd arranged for the one wire deposit of $173,000 and, after paying for the M5, including shipping to the U.S., the remaining funds were almost $72,000. He laughed at his scheme—that Chase Bank manager Hurley, and the credit card companies would be aghast if he didn't refund the money. He imagined the conversation.

Hurley would ask, "What do you mean, that's not your signature?"

"That's right, It's not my signature." Concern would be plastered on Alex's face. "Someone stole a batch of checkbooks out of my mailbox and I have no idea who wrote the check."

"Did you report it to the police?"

"Well, the super reported that all the mailboxes were broken into but he didn't know what was missing. I was traveling; I just returned yesterday." Spinoza smiled; if this had been the only sting, he could have paid some drunk to take a sledge hammer to all the mailboxes.

Visa and the other credit card companies would be incredulous and they'd contact the police. Three $35,000 charges would be rather large to swallow. It would be touch and go, too, when he'd have to deal with those idiots in the Westchester County DA's Fraud Office, but eventually they'd agree—after all, it would be a case of identity theft. All the credit card charges would be reversed.

But this was an experiment. Jesus, he thought, they might drop dead when he made the big hit. They'd never find him after he scored the $7 Million.

Alex returned his attention to the road and saw the sign for the turn-off to Baden-Baden.

●●●

The phone rang in room 35 at the Brenner Park Hotel.

"Hello, is Jutta there? This is Ingrid, her sister." Alex handed the phone with an inquisitive look to Jutta, who mouthed: "I called her from Munich to tell her where we'd be staying."

Jutta said; "*Gruss Gott.*" As she listened, her face blanched. "My God, Ingrid says my husband is on the way here and he has a gun!"

"Your husband? You're married? How'd he find out?"

"Ingrid must have told him."

"But why would she do that?" Spinoza's first reaction was fear, then disbelief followed by suspicion.

"She's always hated me! You better leave, right now!"

"But a gun? Don't they have laws against guns in Germany?"

"He's a policeman in the *Bundes-kriminalamt*, the German Criminal Police. He has a temper. You better get going!"

Spinoza wondered if he was being scammed—but Jutta seemed scared. Flustered and nervous, he threw his clothes in his bag, and ran for the elevator. Descending, he wondered if he would get out of the hotel before Jutta's husband arrived. When the doors opened, he gasped. In front of him was a man breathing hard and excited. Spinoza felt his stomach churn but, after a moment of panic, he realized he was looking at his own reflection in the mirror which was mounted on the wall opposite the elevator doors.

Goddamn it, he thought, I got to get control of myself. It's time to get out of Germany. Alex got back on the autobahn heading for Antwerp, the drop point for shipment of cars to the U.S. He wondered if he'd ever see Jutta again. Was she working him? Still, he reflected, it was a wild time—except for that dog—and he was set for the big one.

●●●

Spinoza returned to New York and closed out the books on the test. $101,000 had gone to BMW for the car and he wired instructions to PokerPlayerOnLine. com to transfer that amount from a new war chest he'd been building to

Frankfurt. He wired $68,000 to Chase Manhattan Bank to cover the check he'd written, and wrote Eurocheques based on the deposits from the poker accounts to retire the $105,000 in debt with the three credit card companies, thus reinforcing their computers' senses of security on the bogus accounts. With these transactions, he was out only the cost of the car and the pending charges for the trip to Germany. The title for the car was in the new duplicate identity; he decided to leave it since a transfer would incur real sales taxes in New York. There was some risk, if he got stopped by the cops, but that would only last a few months and besides, he had his regular drivers' license in the same name.

Four weeks later, when the car arrived, Spinoza took his wife, who'd been unusually distant, for a ride. His plan to steal the $7 Million was afoot but he needed a few more months to pull it off. He figured he may as well keep peace during the interim—like the Phony War before World War II.

"So what do you think of it?" He looked concerned but Alex really didn't care if she liked it. He was just covering his tracks on the trip to Germany. "I had to wait several days to pick it up at the factory."

"How much was it?" asked his wife. "It's beautiful but I thought we'd agreed we were going to save for the children. What did you need another car for anyway?"

Spinoza didn't care whether he left his kids a dime but Dolores had always been anxious to build a nest egg for them. But, when he looked over, Dolores was looking out the window. He began to talk again but she didn't seem to be listening.

"What is it, Dolores? You've been a bitch since I came home from Europe."

"Me? You're in Europe screwing your brains out and you're accusing me?"

"Screwing? What are you talking about?"

"Alex, spare me your bullshit. I know you were doing it with that banker's assistant too."

"What?" Spinoza was stunned. "What do you mean?"

"I signed the Line of Credit, remember? I saw how you looked at her—what's her name, Kathryn?"

"I just looked, that's all. But I thought we had an understanding—what I do overseas doesn't count."

"Well, sure—except now I have an understanding, too—what I do when you're overseas doesn't count either."

"What do you mean? You went out? With who?"

"Oh, Alex, you're such a fool. I've been dating Fred Kappler for months; ever since you started banging Kathryn and spending all your time on-line with that silly poker."

"The car dealer? That asshole?"

"Yes, that asshole—he's more a man than you are. We met at that party at the Eagles. I bought my Prius from him, remember?"

Alex down shifted his M5 into second gear, hit the "Sport" button, and pushed the car up to one hundred miles per hour on the Saw Mill Parkway, red-lining the engine. His hands clutched the steering wheel while he slowly calmed down. Funny, he thought, he was leaving her as soon as he could, but he was going to get Kappler anyway. His lips curled.

●●●

Kappler owned a Toyota Agency on the West Side of Manhattan and belonged to the Brotherhood of the Eagles, just like Alex. Kappler was serious about the Order, but Spinoza had joined just to troll for customers. Fred loved the Eagles and enjoyed the comradeship, health club facilities and dining at the Manhattan Lodge twice a week. The rage for fuel-efficient cars, such as the Prius, had made him a small fortune and he'd volunteered to run for office as a trustee. The trustees controlled the assets of the Lodge and Kappler looked forward to doing his best and making a significant management contribution. But he was worried about his relationship with Dolores Spinoza. She struck him as volatile and Fred feared Alex, or worse, his own wife, would discover his duplicity.

To make it up to his wife, after the election, Fred planned a vacation trip to his ancestral home in Bad Herrenalb, not far from Baden-Baden. His uncle was the day manager at the Hotel Belle Epoque in Baden-Baden and Fred thought his wife would enjoy some time in Germany; she'd been raised in Flensburg, in the north. But first, he had to win the election scheduled for the following month.

●●●

At first, the campaign went well. Fred played handball with a bunch of guys and they all agreed to vote for him. The bridge and gin-rummy players signed on as well. The gang in the bar was more distant; Fred wasn't much of a drinker and the bar was mostly unfamiliar territory for him. He'd resolved to spend more time in the bar when someone began posting flyers all over the lodge, on the walls, bulletin boards, and inside and outside of the doors campaigning for Fred's competitor. Some of the flyers said Fred was a poor manager, too young, some said he was too old, some argued he had insufficient experience, and a few said he carried too much political baggage. One particularly nasty flyer said he drank too much, wasn't social enough, and made too much noise rolling dice for drinks in the bar. It was a recipe for everyone.

On the night of the election, one of Kappler's friends saw Alex Spinoza handing out crib sheets instructing Eagles how to vote. Fred was pretty sure the stuff violated the Eagles rules. But the older members he'd asked about the flyers had told him that it had always been done that way. Still, Fred had thought that such campaigning was déclassé.

The lodge built in 1935 at the corner of Eighth Avenue and 70th Street was incorporated into an old brownstone and adjacent warehouse which had been converted into a health club, including a basketball court, banquet hall, and racquetball and handball courts. The brownstone housed a magnificent old mahogany bar on the ground level. It was crowded with members the night of the election. Fred saw a bunch of his cronies and customers at one of the side tables and ambled over.

"Fred," said a past president (PP) of the Eagles, "good luck in the election."

"Right on," said Barry Wright, the vice president of the lodge. Barry was a close friend who knew about Fred's liaison with Dolores Spinoza. "You'll need it! I saw Alex Spinoza passing out crib sheets telling people how to vote."

"So it's Alex, huh? You can imagine what I'd call him if it wasn't Conduct Unbecoming an Eagle." Fred was bluffing; he worried his wife would hear about Alex and wonder what his problem was.

"Hey," said Barry, "he also had some wild adventure with some babe in Germany. Did you see that photo he showed around of him and a redhead at a fancy hotel in Baden-Baden? He said he picked her up on the flight to get his new car."

"But he's married," said the PP.

"Yeah," said Barry "but when did that stop some people?" He looked at Fred with a wry look. "Besides, Alex must be dumber than a stone to brag about it."

"Did you see all the new members here?" asked Lloyd, one of the oldest members of the lodge. "I haven't seen any of them since they were initiated. I heard that they're here for the election—someone sent them an e-mail telling them their votes were essential to preserve the order of things."

"Shit! Who sent the e-mail?" asked Fred, who still felt a twinge of guilt over Barry's comment.

"We don't know. I just heard rumors. Apparently it was a confidential message."

"My money is on Alex." Barry looked at Fred, shook his head, and smiled.

"Tammany Hall could learn something from this asshole, bringing outside issues into this election," muttered Fred, as he walked through a gauntlet of Eagles who passed out crib sheets in the lobby for the election.

•••

Fred Kappler lost the election eighty votes to thirty-five. He figured about fifty of the voters were new members who'd been enticed to the meeting by the e-mail—otherwise it would have been a close election. Two days later, Barry forwarded him an attachment to an e-mail message:

> From: Barry Wright (*barwrt@earthlink.net*)
> To: Fred Kappler (*Kappler.fred@aol.com*)
> Subject: FW: e-mail in election
> Attachments: ¤ WE NEED YOUR VOTE.txt (30 KB)
> Attached is the e-mail that was circulated to the new members in the Lodge. It turns out I was right. Spinoza was the author. Have you considered poking it somewhere else? Take care. Barry.

Fred read the attachment and saw red. It contained an exhortation to vote if the voter wanted to keep the things he "deserved," like a pool. It went on to explain that Fred didn't have enough experience and that the recipient should spread the word but, in some twisted logic, asked the recipient to keep the message confidential. Kappler clenched his fists. This was too much—he wondered how a philandering jerk like Spinoza could get so resentful over the same thing. Fred swore he'd get even with the SOB.

First, he checked out Alex's credit ratings. For that he needed Spinoza's social security number. No problem, he thought. Alex's wife had bought a Prius at Kappler Toyota and Fred had all the data. He pulled up the website for ABC Credit Data Bureau. Funny, he thought, there were two Alex Spinoza's with two social security numbers and two sets of Visa, MasterCard and Discover accounts. On one of the accounts, three charges for $35,000 had been processed, and then settled. A $68,000 check drawn on Chase Manhattan Bank also caught Fred's attention.

Ernie had an excellent credit rating of 775—not surprising, he was a wealthy man. But a series of payments to jamaicaprocessing.com were interesting. The other Alex Spinoza had an Eurocard account in Frankfurt but Fred couldn't get the details on that account. He picked up the phone and called Barry Wright.

"It's me. Did you ever hear of jamaicaprocessing.com?"

"No. Where is it, Jamaica?"

"No, it's incorporated in the Isle of Man in the English Channel; some place with tight banking restrictions about privacy. But listen, Alex sure seems to like Germany. Do you remember where he stayed in Baden-Baden?"

"Yeah," replied Barry, "he was bragging about the Brenner Park. It's very expensive. Why?"

"I'm doing a little research. Brenner Park, eh? I know the manager at another hotel there; I want to check him out."

"Looking for revenge? Be careful. Maybe he rigged the election for the same reason."

"Barry, I'm gonna get him. I don't know how yet."

"Good luck. Give him one for me."

"My wife and I are going back to Germany for a vacation. We'll spend some time in Offenburg and Bad Herrenalb. Then I'm dropping into Baden-Baden for some research. I'll let you know what happens."

●●●

Kappler drove from Bad Herrenalb to Baden-Baden. The road twisted as it crossed the Murg River and he entered town from the east. Fred's uncle, Manfred Kappler, the manager of the Hotel Belle Epoque, awaited him in the hotel's restaurant. The Belle Epoque sat in a "New Renaissance Village" south of the central district of Baden-Baden, only four hundred meters from the Hotel Brenner Park.

Manfred waved Fred over to his table. After the usual greetings and a magnificent lunch of *Blutwurst* (blood sausage) and *spaetzle*, Manfred pulled an envelope out of his jacket.

"At your request, I asked the manager at the Brenner Park to make a copy of Herr Spinoza's bill. This is highly irregular considering Germany's privacy laws—you must keep this confidential." He handed it to Fred.

"*Vielen dank, Onkel.*" Fred examined the statement and saw that it had a large room service charge and a huge transfer to the Baden-Baden casino cashier, against a Eurocard issued by Deutsche Bank. It was the same account listed in the credit report that he'd run on Spinoza.

"What's this charge to Deutsche Bank? I know it's possible for Americans to get Eurocards but they're unusual and the balances in overseas bank accounts must be reported to the U.S. Treasury."

"I was surprised too, so I called *Herr Direktor* Mannig at Deutsche Bank—I went to school with him in Karlsruhe—and he sent me this document. Manfred produced a faxed page that listed detailed transactions on Spinoza's Eurocard account. "This is even more sensitive so please be careful with it."

Fred smiled at his uncle's initiative and studied the document. It listed one deposit; $173,000 from an unspecified financial organization on the Isle of Man. Fred reached for his beer and did a rapid calculation: three times $35,000 plus $68,000 equaled $173,000. But there were large current charges, about $287,000, incurred at the Brenner Park. So Alex was a gambler besides being an asshole, concluded Fred.

"*Danke sehr, Onkel Manfred. Du hast meinen Tag gemacht.* (Many thanks, Uncle. You've made my day.)

• • •

Fred pondered what to do about Alex. What, he wondered, would be just revenge? He could get him kicked out of the Eagles—such behavior in the election was considered ample grounds. Or, he could exact some other penalty; something more satisfying on a personal basis. Driving to the Frankfurt airport on the return trip, it struck him—the perfect twist to the vignette—he would turn the tables on Spinoza.

• • •

Three weeks later, Fred pulled into the parking lot under the warehouse wing of the Eagles Lodge. Spinoza was climbing out of his M5.

"Fred. You have new wheels?" Alex loved his M5 but Fred, he noted, was driving a brand new Lexus LS460L, the top of the line.

"You like it? It's a great car. I got it through my agency and it costs a bundle—about $85K at the curb with my dealer discount. But I came into some money from the old country so I figured it was time to upgrade. See ya!"

• • •

Alex Spinoza sat at his desk in his second floor home study in Westchester. Tiffany, his wife's Persian cat, jumped up on his desk and circled around a few times before she lay spread-eagled on his desk, in a pool of sunlight that streamed through the open window. He hated that cat almost as much as that goddamn German Chihuahua, Sigmund

Alex was ready for the big score. He planned on writing the first check for $675,000 to jamaicaprocess.com, to be followed by five more, plus credit card transfers. The M5 was packed, ready to go. He was cleaning up his last paperwork and rifled through the usual collection of junk mail, looking for something interesting. An envelope with *Luftpost* markings caught his eye, the monthly statement for his Eurocard account from Deutsche Bank. It showed a charge for $85,350 for a Lexus purchased from Kappler Toyota and an $287,065 charge at the Brenner Park Hotel. The balance was *minus* $372,415! Bile rose as he realized the identity he'd stolen from himself had been stolen by Kappler, that prick! First Kappler had bagged his wife, and now he'd ripped off a car. But what the hell was the charge for $287K? He picked up the phone and called the Brenner Park Hotel.

Alex cradled the phone. The bitch in Germany, Jutta, had ripped him off too! He'd forgotten that when he checked into the Brenner Park he'd authorized the desk to advance funds for charges at the Casino. Jutta, and probably her husband, or sister, had pissed away $250,000 playing roulette. He owed Deutsche Bank money! Big bucks! And there was no way he could chase Kappler; not with that phony second identity. Spinoza grabbed his letter opener, jabbed it into the cat's tail, and then picked up the animal, blade and all, and threw it out the window of his office—the cat shrieking and yowling all the way down to the yard.